The Yacoubian
Building

The Yacoubian Building

Alaa Al Aswany

Translated by
Humphrey Davies

The American University in Cairo Press
Cairo   New York

First published in 2004 by
The American University in Cairo Press
113 Sharia Kasr el Aini, Cairo, Egypt
420 Fifth Avenue, New York 10018
www.aucpress.com

Fifth printing 2005

English translation copyright © 2004 by Humphrey Davies

Copyright © 2002 by Alaa Al Aswany
First published in Arabic in 2002 as 'Imarat Ya'qubyan
Protected under the Berne Convention

Dar el Kutub No. 7952/04
ISBN 977 424 862 7

Designed by Fatiha Bouzidi/AUC Press Design Center
Printed in Egypt

To My Guardian Angel—Iman Taymur

Acknowledgments

This novel would not have seen the light without the help of many friends, first among whom is my friend and teacher Alaa el Deeb, to whom I owe the credit for anything I have achieved in the field of literature. Next are Gamal al-Ghitani, who courageously undertook the publication of the novel in *Akhbar al-adab*, and Dr. Galal Amin, who adopted it enthusiastically and recommended it to the publishers. Likewise, I cannot forget the kindness of Bilal Fadl, Khalid al Sirgani, Ragab Hassan, Makkawi Sa'id, Mahmoud el Wardani, and Muhammad Ibraheem Mabruk, to all of whom I extend my thanks and gratitude.

Translator's Note

Alaa Al Aswany, born in 1957 and a dentist by profession, has written from an early age. His published works include novels, short stories, and a novella, as well as prolific contributions on literature, politics, and social issues to newspapers and magazines covering the political spectrum. *The Yacoubian Building* is his second published novel. Since appearing in 2002, it has gone through several editions and was the best selling Arabic novel for the years 2002 and 2003. It was voted Best Novel for 2003 by listeners to Egypt's Middle East Broadcasting service.

The Yacoubian Building exists, at the address given in the novel. Indeed, it was there that the author's father (Abbas Al Aswany, himself a noted author and winner of the State Prize for Literature for 1974) maintained an office, and there that the author opened his first dental clinic. However, a wanderer on Cairo's Suleiman Basha Street will notice that the real Yacoubian Building does not match its literary namesake in every detail: rather than being in "the high European style" and boasting "balconies decorated with Greek faces carved from stone," it is a restrained albeit elegant exercise in art deco, innocent of balconies. Similarly, the real Halegian's Bar is situated on Abd el Khaliq Sarwat Street, rather than Antikkhana Street. The same logic applies to the characters: while many Egyptian readers believe they know who a given character "really" is, few are portraits from life and in most cases a number of originals have contributed aspects to them. Likewise, the reader need not pay too much heed to the fact that the events described nominally take place before and during Iraq's 1990 invasion of Kuwait: the novel reflects the Egypt of the present.

It would be a mistake, in other words, to assume that everything mentioned in *The Yacoubian Building* is an exact portrait of an identifiable existing original. While the world of the book is undeniably that of today's Egypt, the author achieves this sense of verisimilitude by taking recognizable features from multiple known originals to form new creations. That these collages are so convincing is a measure of the novel's genius and explains in part its appeal.

Inevitably, the book contains numerous references to people and events that are likely to be unfamiliar to the non-Egyptian reader. These are explained in the Glossary at the end of the book. Quotations from the Qur'an are italicized and Arberry's translation has been used (Arthur J. Arberry, *The Koran Interpreted*, Oxford University Press, 1998); a list of references follows the Glossary.

While taking full responsibility for any errors, the translator acknowledges his debt to Siham Abdel Salam, Jacinthe Assaad, Madiha Doss, Maria Golia, Fawzi Mansour, A. Rushdi Nasef, Sayed Ragab, Diya Rashwan, and, above all, the author for help on various aspects of the text.

This translation is dedicated to Gasim.

The Yacoubian Building

1

The distance between Baehler Passage, where Zaki Bey el Dessouki lives, and his office in the Yacoubian Building is not more than a hundred meters, but it takes him an hour to cover it each morning as he is obliged to greet his friends on the street. Clothing- and shoe-store owners, their employees (of both sexes), waiters, cinema staff, habitués of the Brazilian Coffee Stores, even doorkeepers, shoeshine men, beggars, and traffic cops—Zaki Bey knows them all by name and exchanges greetings and news with them. Zaki Bey is one of the oldest residents of Suleiman Basha Street, to which he came in the late 1940s after his return from his studies in France and which he has never thereafter left. To the residents of the street he cuts a well-loved, folkloric figure when he appears before them in his three-piece suit (winter and summer, its bagginess hiding his tiny, emaciated body); with his carefully ironed handkerchief always dangling from his jacket pocket and always of the same color as his tie; with his celebrated cigar, which, in his glory days, was Cuban deluxe but is now of the foul-smelling, tightly-packed, low-quality local kind; and with his old, wrinkled face, his thick glasses, his gleaming false teeth, and his dyed black hair, whose few locks are arranged in rows from the leftmost to the rightmost side of his head in the hope of covering the broad, naked, bald patch. In brief, Zaki Bey el Dessouki is something of a legend, which makes his presence both much looked for and completely unreal, as though he might disappear at any moment, or as though he were an actor playing a part, of whom it is understood that once done he will take off his costume and put his original clothes back on. If we add to the above his jolly temperament, his unceasing stream of scabrous jokes, and his amazing ability to engage in conversation anyone he meets as though he were an old friend, we will understand the secret of the warm welcome with which everyone on the street greets him. Indeed Zaki Bey has only to appear at the top end of the street at around ten in the morning for the salutations to ring out from every side, and often a number of his disciples among the young men who work in the stores will rush up to him to ask him jokingly about certain sexual matters that remain obscure to them, in which case Zaki Bey will draw on his vast and encyclopedic knowledge of the subject to explain to the youths—in great detail, with the utmost pleasure, and in a voice audible to all—the most subtle sexual secrets. Sometimes, in fact, he will ask for a pen and paper (provided in the twinkling of an eye) so that he can draw clearly for the young men some curious coital position that he himself tried in the days of his youth.

Some important information on Zaki Bey el Dessouki should be provided. He is the youngest son of Abd el Aal Basha el Dessouki, the well-known pillar of the Wafd who was prime minister on more than one occasion and was one of the richest men before the Revolution, he and his family owning more than five thousand feddans of prime agricultural land.

Zaki Bey studied engineering in Paris. It had been expected, of course, that he would play a leading political role in Egypt using his father's influence and wealth but suddenly the Revolution erupted and everything changed. Abd el Aal Basha was arrested and brought before the revolutionary tribunal and, though the charge of political corruption failed to stick, he remained in detention for a while and most of his possessions were confiscated and distributed among the peasants under the land reform. Under the impact of all this the Basha soon died, the father's misfortune leaving its mark also on the son. The engineering office that he opened in the Yacoubian Building quickly failed and was transformed with time into the place where Zaki Bey spends his free time each day reading the newspapers, drinking coffee, meeting friends and lovers, or sitting for hours on the balcony contemplating the passersby and traffic on Suleiman Basha.

It must be said, however, that the failure that Engineer Zaki el Dessouki has met with in his professional life should not be attributed entirely to the Revolution; it stems rather, at base, from the feebleness of his ambition and his obsession with sensual pleasure. Indeed his life, which has lasted sixty-five years so far, revolves with all its comings and goings both happy and painful almost entirely around one word—women. He is one of those who fall completely and hopelessly into the sweet clutches of captivity of the female and for whom women are not a lust that flares up and, once satisfied, is extinguished, but an entire world of fascination that constantly renews itself in images of infinitely alluring diversity—the firm, voluptuous bosoms with swelling nipples like delicious grapes; the backsides, pliable and soft, quivering as though in anticipation of his violent assault from behind; the painted lips that drink kisses and moan with pleasure; the hair in all its manifestations (long, straight, and demure, or long and wild with disordered tresses, or medium-length, domestic and well-settled, or that short hair *à la garçon* that evokes unfamiliar, boyish kinds of sex). And the eyes . . . ah, how lovely are the looks from those eyes—honest, or dissimulating and duplicitous; bold or demure; even furious, reproachful, and filled with loathing!

So much and even more did Zaki Bey love women. He had known every kind, starting with Lady Kamla, daughter of the former king's maternal uncle, with whom he learned the etiquette and rites of the royal bed chambers—the candles that burn all night, the glasses of French wine that kindle the flames of desire and obliterate fear, the hot bath before the assignation, when the body is anointed with creams and perfumes. From Lady Kamla (she of the inexorable appetite) he learned how to start and when to desist and how to ask for the most abandoned sexual positions in extremely refined French. Zaki Bey has also slept with women of all classes—oriental dancers, foreigners, society ladies and the wives of the eminent and distinguished, university and secondary school students, even fallen women, peasant women, and housemaids. Every one had her special flavor, and he would often laughingly compare the bedding of Lady Kamla with its rules of protocol and that of that beggar woman he picked up one night when drunk in his Buick and took back to his apartment in Baehler Passage, and whom he discovered, when he went into the bathroom with her to wash her body himself, to be so poor that she made her underwear out of empty cement sacks. He can still remember, with a mixture of tenderness and distress, the woman's embarrassment as she took off her bloomers, on which was written in large letters "Portland Cement—Tura." He remembers too that she was one of the most beautiful of all the women he has known and one of the most ardent in love.

All these varied and teeming experiences have made of Zaki el Dessouki a true expert on women, and in "the science of women," as he calls it, he has strange and eccentric theories that, whether one accepts or rejects them, definitely deserve consideration. Thus he believes for example that the outstandingly lovely woman is usually a cold lover in bed, while women of middling beauty or even of a certain degree of ugliness are always more passionate because they are truly in need of love and will make every effort in their power to please their lovers. Zaki Bey also believes that how a woman pronounces the letter "s"—specifically—is a clue as to how ardent she will be when making love. Thus, if a woman says a word such as "Susu" or "basbusa," for example, in a tremulous, arousing way, he concludes immediately that she is gifted in bed, and that the opposite will also

6

be true. Zaki Bey also believes that every woman on the face of the earth is surrounded by a sort of ethereal field inhabited by vibrations that though invisible and inaudible can nevertheless be vaguely felt, and that one who has trained himself to read these vibrations can divine the degree to which that woman is sexually satisfied. Thus no matter how respectable and modest the woman, Zaki Bey is able to sense her sexual hunger from the trembling of her voice or her nervous, affectedly exaggerated laugh or even from the warmth radiated by her hand when he shakes it. As for the women who are possessed by a satanic lust that they can never quench (*"les filles de joie,"* as Zaki Bey calls them)—those mysterious women who only feel that they truly exist when in bed and making love and who place no other pleasure in life on the same footing as sex, those unhappy beings fated by virtue of their excessive thirst for pleasure to meet with a terrifying and unavoidable fate—those women, Zaki el Dessouki asserts, are all the same, even though their faces may vary. He will invite any who doubt this fact to inspect the pictures published in the newspapers of women sentenced to be executed for participating with their lovers in the murder of their husbands, saying, "We shall discover—with a little observation—that they all have the same countenance: the lips generally full, sensual, relaxed, and not pressed together; the features thick and libidinous; and the look bright and empty, like that of a hungry animal."

It was Sunday. The stores on Suleiman Basha closed their doors, and the bars and cinemas were full of customers. With its locked stores and old-fashioned, European-style buildings the street seemed dark and empty, as though it were in a sad, romantic, European film. At the start of the day, Shazli, the old doorman, moved his seat from next to the elevator to the sidewalk in front of the Yacoubian Building to watch the people going in and out on their day off.

Zaki el Dessouki got to his office a little before noon and from the first instant Abaskharon, the office servant, took in the situation. After twenty years of working for Zaki Bey, Abaskharon had learned to understand his moods at a single glance, knowing full well what it meant when his master arrived at the office excessively elegantly dressed, the scent of the expensive perfume that he kept for special occasions preceding him, and appeared tense and nervous, standing up, sitting down, walking irritably about, never settling to anything, and hiding his impatience in brusqueness and gruffness—it meant that the bey was expecting his first meeting with a new girlfriend. As a result Abaskharon didn't get angry when the bey started berating him for no reason, but shook his head as one who understands how things stand, quickly finished sweeping the reception room, and then grabbed his wooden crutches and pounded vigorously and rapidly off down the long tiled corridor to the large room where the bey was sitting. In a voice that experience had taught him to make completely neutral, he said, "Do you have a meeting, Excellency? Should I get everything ready, Excellency?"

The bey looked in his direction and contemplated him for an instant as though making up his mind as to the proper tone of voice to use in reply. He looked at Abaskharon's striped flannel gallabiya, torn in numerous places, at his crutches and his amputated leg, at his aged face and the grizzled stubble on his chin, at his cunning, narrow eyes and the familiar unctuous, scared smile that never left him, and said, "Get everything ready for a meeting, quickly."

Thus spoke the bey in brusque tones as he went out onto the balcony. In their common dictionary, "a meeting" meant the bey's spending time alone with a woman in the office, and "everything" referred to certain rites that Abaskharon performed for his master just before the love-making, starting with an injection of imported Tri-B vitamin supplement that he administered to him in the buttock and that hurt him so much each time that he would moan out loud and pour curses on "that ass" Abaskharon for his heavy, brutish touch. This would be followed by a cup of sugarless coffee made of beans spiced with nutmeg that the bey would imbibe slowly while dissolving beneath his tongue a small piece of opium. The rites concluded with the placing of a large plate of salad in the middle of the table next to a bottle of Black Label whisky, two empty glasses, and a metal champagne bucket filled to the brim with ice cubes.

Abaskharon quickly set about getting everything ready while Zaki Bey took a seat on the balcony overlooking Suleiman Basha, lit a cigar, and settled down to watch the passersby. His feelings swung between bounding impatience for the beautiful meeting and promptings of anxiety that his sweetheart Rabab would fail to turn up for the appointment, in which case he would have wasted the entire month of effort that he had expended in pursuit of her. He had been obsessed with her since he first saw her at the Cairo Bar in Tawfikiya Square where she worked as a hostess. She had bewitched him completely and day after day he had gone back to the bar to see her. Describing her to an aged friend, he had said, "She represents the beauty of the common people in all its vulgarity and provocativeness. She looks as though she had just stepped out of one of those paintings by Mahmoud Said." Zaki Bey then expatiated on this to make his meaning clearer to his friend, saying, "Do you remember that maid at home who used to beguile your dreams when you were an adolescent? And of whom it was your dearest wish that you might stick yourself to her soft behind, then grab her tender-skinned breasts with your hands as she washed the dishes at the kitchen sink? And that she would bend over in a way that made you stick to her even more closely and whisper in provocative refusal, before giving herself to you, 'Sir. . . . It's wrong, sir. . . .'? In Rabab I have stumbled onto just such a treasure."

However, stumbling onto a treasure does not necessarily mean possessing it and, for the sake of his beloved Rabab, Zaki Bey had been compelled to put up with numerous annoyances, like having to

spend whole nights in a dirty, cramped, badly lit and poorly ventilated place like the Cairo Bar. He had been almost suffocated by the
crowds and the thick cigarette smoke and had come close to being
deafened by the racket of the sound system that never even for an
instant stopped emitting disgusting, vulgar songs. And that was to say
nothing of the foul-mouthed arguments and fistfights among the
patrons of the establishment, who were a mixture of skilled laborers,
bad types, and foreigners, or of the glasses of foul, stomach-burning
brandy that he was forced to toss down every night and the exorbitant mistakes in the checks to which he turned a blind eye, even leaving a big tip for the house plus another even bigger one that he would
thrust into the cleavage of Rabab's dress, feeling, as soon as his
fingers touched her full, swaying breasts, the hot blood surging in his
veins and a violence of desire that almost hurt him it was so powerful and insistent.

Zaki Bey had put up with all of this for the sake of Rabab, inviting her again and again to meet him outside the bar. She would refuse
coquettishly and he would repeat his invitation, never losing hope,
and then just yesterday she had agreed to visit him at the office. So
overjoyed had he been that he had thrust a fifty-pound note into her
dress without the slightest feeling of regret and she had come up to
him so close that he had felt her hot breath on his face and biting her
lower lip with her teeth she had whispered in a provocative voice that
demolished what equanimity he had left, "Tomorrow, I'll pay you
back, sir . . . for everything you've done for me. . . ."

Zaki Bey bore the painful Tri-B injection, dissolved the opium,
and started slowly drinking the first glass of whisky, followed by a
second and a third, which soon released him from his tension. Good
humor enveloped him and pleasant musings started gently caressing
his head like soft tunes. Rabab's appointment was for one o'clock.
By the time the wall clock struck two, Zaki Bey had almost lost
hope, when suddenly he heard the sound of Abaskharon's crutches

striking the hallway tiles, followed immediately by his face appearing around the door as he said, his voice panting with excitement as though the news genuinely made him happy, "Madame Rabab has arrived, Excellency."

In 1934, Hagop Yacoubian, the millionaire and then doyen of the Armenian community in Egypt, decided to construct an apartment block that would bear his name. He chose for it the best site on Suleiman Basha and engaged a well-known Italian engineering firm to build it, and the firm came up with a beautiful design—ten lofty stories in the high classical European style, the balconies decorated with Greek faces carved in stone, the columns, steps, and corridors all of natural marble, and the latest model of elevator by Schindler. Construction continued for two whole years, at the end of which there emerged an architectural gem that so exceeded expectations that its owner requested of the Italian architect that he inscribe his name, Yacoubian, on the inside of the doorway in large Latin characters that were lit up at night in neon, as though to immortalize his name and emphasize his ownership of the gorgeous building.

The cream of the society of those days took up residence in the Yacoubian Building—ministers, big land-owning bashas, foreign manufacturers, and two Jewish millionaires (one of them belonging to the famous Mosseri family). The ground floor of the building was divided equally between a spacious garage with numerous doors at the back where the residents' cars (most of them luxury makes such as Rolls-Royce, Buick, and Chevrolet) were kept overnight and at the front a large store with three frontages that Yacoubian kept as a showroom for the silver products made in his factories. This showroom remained in business successfully for four decades, then little by little declined, until recently it was bought by Hagg Muhammad Azzam, who re-opened it as a clothing store. On the broad roof two rooms with utilities were set aside for the doorkeeper and his family to live in, while on the other side of the roof fifty small rooms were constructed, one for each apartment in the building. Each of these rooms was no more than two meters by two meters in area and the walls and doors were all of solid iron and locked with padlocks whose keys were handed over to the owners of the apartments. These iron rooms had a variety of uses at that time, such as storing foodstuffs, overnight kenneling for dogs (if they were large or fierce), and laundering clothes, which in those days (before the spread of the electric washing machine) was undertaken by professional washerwomen who would do the wash in the room and hang it out on long lines that extended across the roof. The rooms were never used as places for the servants to sleep, perhaps because the residents of the building at that time were aristocrats and foreigners who could not conceive of the possibility of any human being sleeping in such a cramped place. Instead, they would set aside a room in their ample, luxurious apartments (which sometimes contained eight or ten rooms on two levels joined by an internal stairway) for the servants.

In 1952 the Revolution came and everything changed. The exodus of Jews and foreigners from Egypt started and every apartment that was vacated by reason of the departure of its owners was taken over by an officer of the armed forces, who were the influential people of the time. By the 1960s, half the apartments were lived in by officers of various ranks, from first lieutenants and recently married captains all the way up to generals, who would move into the building with their large families. General El Dakrouri (at one point director of President Muhammad Naguib's office) was even able to acquire two large apartments next door to one another on the tenth floor, one of which he used as a residence for himself and his family, the other as a private office where he would meet petitioners in the afternoon.

The officers' wives began using the iron rooms in a different way: for the first time they were turned into places for the stewards, cooks, and young maids that they brought from their villages to serve their families to stay in. Some of the officers' wives were of plebeian origin and could see nothing wrong in raising small animals (rabbits, ducks, and chickens) in the iron rooms and the West Cairo District's registers saw numerous complaints filed by the old residents to prevent the raising of such animals on the roof. Owing to the officers' pull, however, these always got shelved, until the residents complained to General El Dakrouri, who, thanks to his influence with the former, was able to put a stop to this insanitary phenomenon.

In the seventies came the 'Open Door Policy' and the well-to-do started to leave the downtown area for El Mohandiseen and Medinet Nasr, some of them selling their apartments in the Yacoubian Building, others using them as offices and clinics for their recently graduated sons or renting them furnished to Arab tourists. The result was that the connection between the iron rooms and the building's apartments was gradually severed and the former stewards and servants ceded their iron rooms for money to new, poor residents coming from the countryside or working somewhere downtown who needed a place to live that was close by and cheap.

This transfer of control was made easier by the death of the Armenian agent in charge of the building, Monsieur Grigor, who used to administer the property of the millionaire Hagop Yacoubian with the utmost honesty and accuracy, sending the proceeds in December of each year to Switzerland, where Yacoubian's heirs had migrated after the Revolution. Grigor was succeeded as agent by Maître Fikri Abd el Shaheed, the lawyer, who would do anything provided he was paid, taking, for example, one large percentage from the former occupant of the iron room and another from the new tenant for writing him a contract for the room.

The final outcome was the growth of a new community on the roof that was entirely independent of the rest of the building. Some of the newcomers rented two rooms next to one another and made a small residence out of them with all utilities (latrine and washroom), while others, the poorest, collaborated to create a shared latrine for every three or four rooms, the roof community thus coming to resemble any other popular community in Egypt. The children run around all over the roof barefoot and half naked and the women spend the day cooking, holding gossip sessions in the sun, and, frequently, quarreling, at which moments they will exchange the grossest insults as well as accusations touching on one another's honor, only to make up soon after and behave with complete good will toward one another as though nothing has happened. Indeed, they will plant hot, lip-smacking kisses on each other's cheeks and even weep from excess of sentiment and affection.

The men pay little attention to the women's quarrels, viewing them as just one more indication of that defectiveness of mind of which the Prophet—God bless him and grant him peace—spoke. These men of the roof pass their days in a bitter and wearisome struggle to earn a living and return at the end of the day exhausted and in a hurry to partake of their small pleasures—tasty hot food and a few pipes of tobacco (or of hashish if they have the money), which they either smoke in a waterpipe on their own or stay up to smoke while talking with the others on the roof on summer nights. The third pleasure is sex, in which the people of the roof revel and which they see nothing wrong with discussing frankly so long as it is of a sort sanctioned by religion. Here there is a contradiction. Any of the men of the roof would be ashamed, like most lower-class people, to mention his wife by name in front of the others, referring to her as "Mother of So-and-so," or "the kids," as in "the kids cooked mulukhiya today," the company understanding that he means his wife. This same man, however, will feel no embarrassment at mentioning, in a gathering of other men, the most precise details of his private relations with his wife, so that the men of the roof come to know almost everything of one another's sexual activities. As for the women, and without regard for their degree of religiosity or morality, they all love sex enormously and will whisper the secrets of the bed to one another, followed, if they are on their own, by bursts of laughter that are carefree or even obscene. They do not love it simply as a way of quenching lust but because sex, and their husbands' greed for it, makes them feel that despite all the misery they suffer, they are still women, beautiful and desired by their menfolk. At that certain moment when the children are asleep, having had their dinner and given praise to their Lord, and there is enough food in the house to last for a week or more, and there is a little money set aside for emergencies, and the room they all live in is clean and tidy, and the husband has come home on Thursday night in a good mood because of the effect of the hashish and asked for his wife, is it not then her duty to obey his call, after first bathing, prettying herself up, and putting on perfume? Do these brief hours of pleasure not furnish her with proof that her wretched life is somehow, despite everything, blessed with success? It would take a skilled painter to convey to us the expressions on the face of a woman on the roof of a Friday morning, when, after her husband has gone down to perform the prayer and she has washed off the traces of love-making, she emerges to hang out the washed bedding—at that moment, with her wet hair, her flushed complexion, and the serene expression in her eyes, she looks like a rose that, watered with the dew of the morning, has arrived at the peak of its perfection.

The darkness of night was receding, heralding a new morning, and a dim, small light on the roof shone from the window of the room belonging to Shazli the doorkeeper, where his teenage son Taha had spent the night sleepless with anxiety. Now he performed the dawn prayer plus the two superrogatory prostrations, then sat on the bed in his white gallabiya reading from *The Book of Answered Prayer* and repeating in a frail whisper in the silence of the room, "O God, I ask

You for whatever good this day may hold and I take refuge with You from whatever evil it may hold and from any evil I may meet within it. O God, watch over me with Your eye that never sleeps and forgive me through Your power, that I perish not; You are my hope. My Lord, Master of Majesty and Bounty, to You I direct my face, so bring Your noble face close to me and receive me with Your unalloyed forgiveness and generosity, smiling on me and content with me in Your mercy!"

Taha continued to read the prayers until the light of morning shone into the chamber and little by little life started to stir in the iron rooms—voices, cries, laughter and coughing, doors shutting and opening, and the smell of hot water, tea, coffee, charcoal, and tobacco. For the inhabitants of the roof it was just the start of another day; Taha el Shazli, however, knew that on this day his fate would be decided forever. After a few hours, he would present himself for the character interview at the Police Academy—the last hurdle in the long race of hope. Since childhood, he has dreamed of being a police officer and has devoted all his efforts to realizing that dream. He has applied himself to memorizing everything for the general secondary examination and as a result obtained a score of eighty-nine percent (Humanities) without private tutoring (apart from a few review groups at the school, for which his father had only just been able to come up with the money). During summer vacations he joined the Abdeen Youth Center (for ten pounds a month) and put up with the exhausting body-building exercises in order to acquire the athletic physique that would allow him to pass the physical fitness tests at the Police Academy.

In order to realize this dream, Taha has courted the police officers in the district until they are all his friends, both those of the Kasr el Nil police station and of the Kotzika substation that belongs to it. From them, Taha has learned all the details relating to the admission tests for the police and found out too about the twenty thousand pounds that the well-to-do pay as a bribe to assure their children's acceptance into the college (and how he wishes he possessed such a sum!). In order to realize this dream, Taha el Shazli has also put up with the meanness and the arrogance of the building's inhabitants.

Since he was little he had helped his father run errands for people, and when his intelligence and academic excellence manifested themselves, the inhabitants reacted in different ways. Some encouraged him to study, gave him generous gifts, and prophesied a glorious future for him. Others, however, (and there were many of these) were somehow disturbed by the idea of "the high-flying doorkeeper's son" and tried to convince his father to enroll him in vocational training as soon as he finished intermediary school "so that he can learn a trade that will be of use to you and to himself," as they would say to elderly "Uncle" Shazli, with a show of concern for his welfare. When Taha enrolled in general secondary school and continued to do well, they would send for him on exam days and entrust him with difficult tasks that would take a long time, tipping him generously to tempt him, while concealing a malign desire to keep him from his studies. Taha would accept these tasks because of his need for cash but would go on wearing himself out with study, often going one or two days without sleep.

When the general secondary exam results came out and he obtained a higher score than the children of many in the building, the grumblers started to talk openly. One of them would run into another in front of the elevator and ask him sarcastically if he had offered his congratulations to the doorkeeper on his son's high marks; then he would add bitingly that the doorkeeper's son would soon join the Police Academy and graduate as an officer with two stars on his epaulettes. At this point the other person would candidly reveal his annoyance, first praising Taha's character and his hard work, then going on to say in a serious tone of voice (as though he had the general principle and not the individual in mind) that jobs in the police, the judiciary, and sensitive positions in general should be given only to the children of people who were somebody, because the children

17

of doorkeepers, laundrymen, and such like, if they attained any authority, would use it to compensate for the inferiority complexes and other neuroses they had acquired during their early childhood. Then he would bring his speech to an end by cursing Abd el Nasser, who had introduced free education, or quote as authority the saying of the Prophet—God bless him and grant him peace—"Teach not the children of the lowly!"

These same residents started picking on Taha when the results appeared and finding fault with him for the most trivial of reasons, such as washing the car and forgetting to put the floormats back in place, or being a few minutes late in the performance of an errand to somewhere far away, or buying ten things for them from the market and forgetting one. They would insult him deliberately and unmistakably in order to push him into responding that he would not put up with such insults because he was an educated person, which would be their golden opportunity to announce to him the truth— that here he was a mere doorkeeper, no more and no less, and if he didn't like his job he should leave it to someone who needed it. But Taha never gave them that opportunity. He would meet their outbursts with silence, a bowed head, and a slight smile, his handsome brown face at these moments giving the impression that he did not agree with what was directed at him and that it was entirely in his power to rebut the insult but that respect for the other's greater age prevented him from so doing.

This was one of a number of fall-back positions, tantamount to defensive tactics, that Taha used under difficult circumstances in order to express what he felt while at the same time avoiding problems, positions that had initially been a matter of acting for him but which he soon performed sincerely and as though they were the truth. For example, he did not like to sit on the doorkeeper's bench so that he had to get up respectfully for every resident, and if he was sitting on the bench and he saw a resident coming, he would busy himself with something that would obviate his duty to stand up. Similarly, he was accustomed to addressing the residents with a carefully calculated modicum of respect and to treating them as an employee would his superior, and not as a servant his master. As for the children of the residents who were close to him in age, he treated them as complete equals. He would call them by their first names and converse and play around with them like close friends, borrowing from them school books that he might not actually need in order to remind them that despite his position as a doorkeeper he was their colleague when it came to study.

These were the commonplaces of his day-to-day life—poverty, back-breaking hard work, the arrogance of the residents, and the five-pound note, always folded, that his father bestowed on him every Saturday and on which he practiced every stratagem to make last the whole week; the smooth, warm hand of a resident extended lazily and graciously from a car window to give him a tip (at the sight of which he had to raise his hand in a military-style salute and thank his benefactor enthusiastically and audibly); that look, impertinent and full of smugness or covertly sympathetic and tolerant, inspired by embarrassment at the "issue," which he noted in the eyes of his school friends when they visited him and discovered that he lived in the doorkeeper's quarters "up on the roof"; that hateful, embarrassing question "Are you the doorkeeper?" that strangers to the building addressed to him; and the deliberate slowing down of the residents as they entered the building so that he would hurry to relieve them of whatever they were carrying no matter how light or unimportant.

It is with annoyances such as these that the day passes, but when Taha gets into bed at the end of the evening it is always in a state of purity and with his ablutions made, after he has first performed the evening prayer, plus superrogatory odd and even series of prostrations. Then he stares long into the darkness of the room, gradually soaring until he beholds himself in his mind's eye as a police officer strutting proudly in his beautiful uniform with the brass stars gleaming on his shoulder and the impressive government-issue pistol dangling from his belt. He imagines that he has married his sweetheart Busayna el Sayed and that they have moved to a suitable apartment in an up-market district far from the noise and dirt of the roof.

He firmly believed that God would make all his dreams come true—first of all because he made the utmost effort to honor God's commandments, observing the obligatory prayers and avoiding major sins (and God had given to the observant in a noble verse of the Qur'an the good news that *Had the people of the cities believed and been god-fearing, We would have opened upon them blessings from heaven and earth*) and second because he had the highest expectations of God's good intentions (given that the Almighty and Glorious had said, in words revealed to the Prophet, "I am according to my slaves' expectations of me: if good, then good, and if bad, then bad"). And see— God had fulfilled his promise and granted him success in the general secondary exams, and he had passed, praise God, all the tests for the Police College. All that remained for him to do was the character interview, which he would pass that same day, God willing.

Taha rose and prayed the two morning prostrations, plus two more in supplication for the achievement of his wish, then washed, shaved, and began to get dressed. He had bought a new gray suit, a shining white shirt, and a beautiful blue tie for the character interview and when he glanced at himself for the last time in the mirror, he looked very smart. As he kissed his mother goodbye, she put her hand on his head muttering an incantation, then started praying for him with an ardor that made his heart pound. In the lobby of the building, he found his father sitting with his legs tucked up under him on the bench as was his habit. The old man rose slowly and looked at Taha for a moment. Then he put his hand on his shoulder and smiled, his white moustache quivering and revealing his toothless mouth, and he said proudly, "Congratulations in advance, Mr. Officer!"

It was past ten o'clock and Suleiman Basha was crowded with cars and pedestrians and most of the stores had opened their doors. It occurred to Taha that he had a whole hour ahead of him before the exam and he decided that he would take a cab for fear of spoiling his suit on the crowded buses. He wished he could spend the remaining time with Busayna. Their agreed method was that he should pass in front of the Shanan clothing store where she worked; when she saw him she would ask permission from Mr. Talal, the owner, to leave, using the excuse that she had to fetch something or other from the storeroom, and then catch up with him at their favorite place in the new garden in Tawfikiya Square.

Taha did the usual routine and sat there for about a quarter of an hour before Busayna appeared. At the sight of her, he felt his heart beating hard. He loved the way she walked, moving with small, slow steps, looking at the ground, and giving the impression that she was embarrassed or for some reason regretful, or was walking over a fragile surface with extreme care, so as not to break it with her footsteps. Noticing that she was wearing the tight-fitting red dress that revealed the details of her body and whose wide and low-cut front showed her full breasts, he experienced a surge of anger and remembered that he had quarreled with her before in an attempt to make her stop wearing it. However, he suppressed his annoyance, not wishing to spoil the occasion, and she smiled, showing her small, white, regular, teeth and the two wonderful dimples on either side of her mouth and lips, which she had painted dark red. She sat down next to him on the low marble garden wall, turned toward him and looked at him with her wide seemingly astonished honey-colored eyes and said, "What a dandy!"

He answered in an urgent whisper, "I'm going for the character interview now and I wanted to see you."

"The Lord be with you!" said Busayna with true tenderness. His heart beat hard and at that moment he wished he could clasp her to his chest.

"Are you scared?" she asked.

"I have placed myself in the hands of God, Almighty and Glorious, and whatever Our Lord may do I shall gladly accept, God willing."

He spoke fast, as though he had prepared the answer ahead of time or as though he were trying to convince himself with his own words. He was silent for a moment, then went on gently, looking into her eyes, "Pray for me."

"The Lord grant you success, Taha," she exclaimed warmly.

Then she went on, as though she thought she had gone too far in showing her feelings, "I have to go now because Mr. Talal is waiting for me."

As she withdrew, he tried to make her stay but she put out her hand and shook his, her eyes avoiding him, and said in an ordinary, formal way, "Best of luck." Later, when he was sitting in the taxi, Taha reflected that Busayna's attitude toward him had changed and there was no point in ignoring it; that he knew her well and that one look was enough for him to penetrate her innermost thoughts. He had memorized everything about her—her face, whether radiant with happiness or sad, her uncertain smile and the way she blushed when she was embarrassed, her wildcat glances and glowering (but still beautiful) features when she was angry; he even loved to look at her when she had just woken up and the traces of sleep were still on her face, making her look like a compliant, gentle-hearted child.

He loved her and he preserved in his memory the image of her as a little girl when she used to play with him on the roof and he used to run after her and deliberately hang on to her so that the smell of soap from her hair would tickle his nose; of her as a student at the commercial secondary school wearing the white shirt, blue skirt, and short white school socks above black shoes as she walked hugging her bag as though to hide her ripening bosom; and the beautiful images of them wandering together at the Barrages and the Zoo, and of the day when they revealed their love to one another and agreed to marry and how after that she had clung to him and asked him questions about the details of his life, as though she were his young wife looking after him. They had agreed on everything for the future, even the number of children they would have and their names and what their first apartment would look like.

Then suddenly she had changed. She had become less interested in him and took to talking about "their project" listlessly and sarcastically. She would often quarrel with him and avoid meeting him, using a variety of excuses. This had happened right after her father died. Why had she changed? Was their love just an adolescent thing, to be grown out of as they got older? Or had she fallen in love with someone else? This last thought pricked him like a thorn till he bled. He started to picture Mr. Talal the Syrian (owner of the store where she worked) taking her arm in his and wearing a wedding suit.

Taha became aware of a heavy worry weighing on his heart, then awoke from his thoughts as the taxi came to a halt in front of the Police College building, which at that moment appeared impressive and historic, as though it were the fortress of fate in which his destiny would be decided. His exam nerves came back to him and he started reciting the Throne Verse in a whisper as he approached the gate.

The information available about Abaskharon in his youth is extremely sparse.

We don't know what he did before the age of forty or the circumstances in which his right leg was amputated. Everything we know starts with that rainy winter's day twenty years ago when Abaskharon arrived at the Yacoubian Building in the black Chevrolet of Madame Sanaa Fanous, a widowed Copt of Upper Egyptian origin, rich, and with two children to whose upbringing she had devoted her life following the death of her husband. Despite her devotion to her children, however, she responded from time to time to the whimsical demands of her body and Zaki el Dessouki had got to know her at the Automobile Club and had been her companion for a while. Much as she enjoyed the relationship, her religious conscience gave her no rest and would often make her break into painful tears as she lay in Zaki's arms after the accomplishment of their pleasure and go and appease her guilt by taking on an abundance of good works through the church. Thus it was that no sooner did Borei, Zaki's former office servant, die than she insisted on his appointing Abaskharon (whose name was on the assistance list at the church) and suddenly there he was, standing hunched up like a mouse and staring at the ground, at his first meeting with Zaki Bey, who was so disappointed at his shabby appearance, his amputated leg, and his crutches, which marked him with the stamp of a beggar, that he said sarcastically to his friend Sanaa in French, "But, my dear, I'm running an office, not a charity!"

She continued trying to win him over with blandishments until in the end he grudgingly agreed to employ Abaskharon, with the idea that he would do what she wanted for a few days then throw him out . . . but here they were! Abaskharon had demonstrated from the first day an unusual competence: he had an uncommon capacity for uninterrupted, exhausting work and even asked the Bey daily to give him new things to add to his list of duties. He also possessed a sharp intelligence, adroitness, and shrewdness, which made him do the right thing in any given situation and with a capacity for absolute discretion, for he would see and hear nothing of what took place in front of him, be it even murder.

By dint of these great virtues before a few months had passed Zaki Bey couldn't do without Abaskharon for so much as an hour. He even had a new bell put in in the kitchen of the apartment so that he could summon him whenever he needed him and he gave him a generous salary and allowed him to stay overnight in the office (which was something he hadn't done with anyone before). Abaskharon for his part had fathomed the Bey's nature from the first day and realized that his master was self-indulgent, a pleasure-seeker, and given to sudden whims and caprices and that his head was rarely free of the effect of narcotics. This sort of man (as per Abaskharon's wide experience of life) was quick to get angry and had a sharp temper but rarely did any harm and the worst that one was likely to suffer from him was verbal abuse or a dressing down. Abaskharon promised himself that he would never argue with or question his master about what he asked for and that he would always take the initiative in apologizing and ingratiating himself, in order to gain his affection. Likewise he never addressed him by any term other than "Excellency," which he would insert into any sentence he uttered. Thus, if the Bey asked him, for example, "What time is it now?" Abaskharon would reply, "Five o'clock, Excellency."

To tell the truth, Abaskharon's adaptation to his work is somewhat reminiscent of a biological phenomenon. Thus in the midst of the quiet darkness that reigns over the apartment during the daylight hours and of the ancient musty smell that emanates from the mixing of the scent of old furniture with that of the damp and of the double-strength carbolic acid that the Bey insists be used to clean the bathroom—in this "medium," when Abaskharon emerges from one of the corners of the apartment with his crutches, his ever-dirty gallabiya, his aged hang-dog face, and his ingratiating smile, he seems like a creature functioning effectively in its natural surroundings, like a fish in water, or a cockroach in the drain. Indeed whenever for some reason he leaves the Yacoubian Building and walks down the sunny street through the passersby and the noise of the cars, he looks odd and out of place, like a bat in daylight, and his integrity is restored only when he returns to the office where he has spent two decades concealed in darkness and damp.

We must not, however, be fooled into thinking of Abaskharon as no more than an obedient servant, for the truth is that there is much more to him than that and behind his servile, weak exterior lies concealed a strong will, and precise goals that he will fight courageously and obstinately to achieve. In addition to the raising and educating of his three daughters, he has taken on his shoulders the care of his younger brother Malak and his children too. This gives us the clue to understanding what he does every evening when, alone in his small room, he extracts from the pocket of his gallabiya every coin and small, sweat-soaked, folded banknote, whether obtained directly as tips or that he has succeeded in filching from the purchases for the office. (Abaskharon's brokering methods may be taken as a model of precise, skilful fraud, for he does not, like an amateur, inflate the prices of what he buys, since the prices are known, or may be known, at any moment. Instead he will for example filch each day from the coffee, tea, and sugar an amount too small to be noticed, then re-package the stolen provisions in new bags and resell them to Zaki Bey, presenting genuine invoices that he has obtained through a private agreement with the pious, bearded Muslim grocer on Marouf Street.)

In the evening, before retiring to his bed, Abaskharon counts his money twice with care, then pulls out the little blue indelible pencil that he always keeps behind his ear and writes down the balance of his earnings, subtracting from them the amount he is going to save (which he will place in his savings account on Sunday and never thereafter touch), then pay off mentally out of the remainder of what he has received the needs of his large family. And whether he has anything left over after that or not, Abaskharon, the believing Christian, cannot sleep until he has chanted the prayer of thanks to the Lord, his voice reverberating in the silence of the night as he whispers with genuine piety before the figure of the crucified Christ that hangs on the kitchen wall, "because, O Lord, Thou hast fed me and fed my children; thus, I praise You as Your name is glorified in Heaven. Amen."

A word, unavoidably, about Malak.

The fingers of the hand differ from one another in appearance but all move together in coordination to carry out a given task. Similarly, on the soccer pitch, the mid-field player shoots the ball with the utmost precision to land at the feet of the striker so that he can score a goal. Abaskharon's relationship with his brother Malak was conducted with the same extraordinary harmony.

Malak learned tailoring in shirt-making workshops when he was young; thus domestic service has not left its stamp of abjection upon him, and the fact is his short stature, his cheap, dark-colored 'people's suit', his huge belly, and his plump face devoid of any good looks leave a disturbing first impression. However, he hastens to take the initiative with anyone he meets by smiling his broad smile and shaking his hand warmly, talking to him like an old friend and concurring with all his opinions (so long as they do not touch his vital interests), then insistently offering him a Cleopatra cigarette from the wrinkled pack that he carefully extracts from his pocket, checking each time that it is okay, as though it were a jewel. This excessive pleasantness has another side to it, however. If necessary Malak will switch, in an instant and with the greatest of ease, to the utterly foul language that is to be expected of someone who has received most of his upbringing on the street. Since he combines two opposites—viciousness and cowardice, the violent desire to hurt his opponents and excessive fear of the consequences—he has become accustomed in his battles to attacking with everything he has. If he finds no resistance, he will go to any lengths in his aggression, without the slightest mercy, as though he doesn't know the meaning of fear. And if he meets with serious resistance from his foe, he will back off immediately without thinking twice. To all these high-level skills of Malak's are added the sagacity and cunning of Abaskharon, so that the two of them work together in perfect coordination and are able, truth to tell, to pull off the most amazing feats.

The two brothers wanted to get a room on the roof, so they had planned and schemed for many months till, on this very day, the hour for action had arrived and no sooner had Rabab entered to see

Zaki Bey than Abaskharon, standing in the doorway, bowed and said with a slight, crafty smile, "Excellency. Your permission to run a quick errand?" Before he had finished the sentence, the Bey (who was preoccupied with his girl friend) had gestured to him to go. Abaskharon closed the door quietly and his face, as his wooden crutches struck the tiles of the hallway, seemed to change. The servile, ingratiating smile disappeared and a serious, anxious expression appeared in its place. Abaskharon made for the small kitchen that was next to the entrance to the apartment and looked around cautiously. Then he stretched up, leaning on a crutch, until he was able carefully to remove the picture of the Virgin that hung on the wall and behind which was a niche. Sticking his hand into this, he pulled out several large bundles of banknotes, which he set about concealing carefully in his vest and pockets. Then he left the apartment, closing the door gently and firmly behind him. Reaching the entrance of the building, he turned, using his crutch, to the right and approached the doorkeeper's room, from which his brother Malak, who had been waiting for him, quickly emerged. The brothers exchanged a single look of understanding and a few minutes later were making their way down Suleiman Basha on their way to the Automobile Club to meet Fikri Abd el Shaheed, the lawyer who was the agent for the Yacoubian Building.

They had prepared themselves for this meeting and talked it over between themselves for a period of months till there was nothing left to discuss. Thus they proceeded in silence, though Abaskharon started to mutter prayers to the Virgin and Christ the Savior to grant them success in their mission. Malak on the other hand was racking his brains for the most effective words with which to open the conversation with Fikri Bey. He had spent the last weeks gathering information about him and was now aware that the man would do anything for money and that he liked drink and women. He had been to meet him at his office on Kasr el Nil Street and presented him with a gift of a bottle of fine Old Parr whisky before opening the subject of the iron room at the entrance to the roof that had been left empty by the death of Atiya, the newspaper seller, who had lived and died unmarried, his room thus reverting to the owner. Malak had been dreaming of opening this room as a shirt shop ever since he had turned thirty and found himself still a journeyman, moving from store to store as circumstances required. When he broached the topic, Fikri Bey asked for time to think and after much pressure from Malak and his brother had agreed to give it to them in return for the sum of six thousand pounds and not a penny less, and had given them an appointment at the Automobile Club, where he was accustomed to take lunch every Sunday. When the brothers reached the club, Abaskharon felt overwhelmed at the grandness of the place and stared at the real marble that covered the walls and the floor and the luxurious red carpet that extended up to the elevator. Malak seemed to sense this and pressed his arm in encouragement, then advanced and warmly shook hands with the doorman of the club, asking him for Fikri Abd el Shaheed. In preparation for this day, Malak had got to know the workers at the Automobile Club over the past two weeks and gained their friendship with kind, flattering words and a few white gallabiyas that he had presented them as gifts. The waiters and workers hastened therefore to welcome the brothers and led them to the restaurant on the second floor where Fikri Bey was taking lunch with a fat white lady friend of his. Naturally, it wouldn't do for the brothers to interrupt the Bey, so they sent someone to him to inform him of their presence and waited for him in a side room.

Only a few minutes passed before Fikri Abd el Shaheed appeared, with his fat body, his large bald patch, and his face ruddy and white as a foreigner's; it became immediately obvious from the redness of his eyes and the slight slur in his speech that he had drunk a lot. After the greetings and compliments Abaskharon launched into a long interlude in praise of the Bey, his kind-hearted-ness, and his similarity in all his doings to Christ. He went on to tell (his brother Malak listening attentively and with affected admira-tion) how the Bey would exempt many of his clients from the costs of cases if he was sure that they had been wronged and were poor and unable to pay.

"Do you know, Malak, what Fikri Bey says to a poor client if he tries to pay?" Having posed the question, Abaskharon quickly answered it himself. "He says, 'Go and prostrate yourself in thanks to the Lord Jesus, for He has paid me the fees for your case in full'!" Malak sucked his lips, folded his hands over his protruding stomach, looked at the ground as though completely overcome, and said, "There you see a true Christian!"

Fikri Bey, however, though drunk, was attentive to the way the conversation was going and did not much like its drift; so to bring matters to a head he said in a no-nonsense tone, "Did you bring the money as agreed?"

"Of course, Your Honor," cried Abaskharon, as he handed him two pieces of paper. "Here's the contract as agreed with Your Honor, and God bless you."

Then he thrust his hand into his vest to pull out the money. He had brought the agreed upon six thousand, but had distributed the notes about his person in order to leave himself room for maneuver. He started by pulling out four thousand pounds and held out his hand with these in it to the Bey, who cried out angrily, "What's that? Where's the rest?" At this, the brothers burst out with one voice, as though singing an aria, into a joint plea—Abaskharon in his hoarse, phlegmy, panting tones and Malak in his sharp, high-pitched, loud ones, their words overlapping until they became incomprehensible, though taken as a whole they were intended to awaken the Bey's sym-pathy by speaking of their poverty and noting that they had, by the Living Christ, gone into debt to get the money and that in all honesty they were unable to pay more than that. Fikri Bey didn't relent for a second. Indeed he got angrier and saying, "This is how children behave! This is no use to me!" he turned around to go back into the restaurant. Abaskharon, however, who had been expecting this move, threw himself so forcefully toward the Bey that he stumbled and was about to fall but with a lightning movement pulled another bundle of notes, worth a thousand pounds, out of the pocket of his gallabiya and thrust it with the other bundles into the pocket of the Bey, who displayed no serious resistance and allowed this to happen. At this Abaskharon was obliged to launch into another interlude of pleading during which he attempted to kiss the Bey's hand more than once and finally brought his ardent importunities to a close with a special move that he kept in reserve for emergencies, suddenly bending his torso backwards and pulling his worn, dirty gallabiya upward with both hands so that his truncated leg, attached to the depressingly dark-colored prosthesis, was displayed. In a hoarse, disjointed, voice designed to evoke pity he shouted, "I'm a cripple, sir, and my leg's gone! A cripple with a parcel of children to look after, and Malak has four children and their mother to support! If you love the Lord Christ, sir, don't turn me away broken-hearted!"

This was more than Fikri Bey could withstand and a little while later the three of them were sitting and signing the contract—Fikri Bey, who was furious at what he afterwards called, as he recounted what had happened to his lady friend, "moral blackmail," Malak, who was thinking about the first steps he would take in his new room on the roof, and Abaskharon, who kept in place on his face his final, affecting expression (a sad, broken look, as though he been vanquished, and subjected to unbearable burdens); inside, however, he was happy both because the rental contract had been signed and because he had managed with his skill to save a one thousand-pound bundle, whose delicious warmth he could feel in the right-hand pocket of his gallabiya.

Downtown remained, for at least a hundred years, the commercial and social center of Cairo, where were situated the biggest banks, the foreign companies, the stores, the clinics and the offices of famous doctors and lawyers, the cinemas, and the luxury restaurants. Egypt's former élite had built the downtown area to be Cairo's European quarter, to the degree that you would find streets that looked the same as those to be found in any of the capitals of Europe, with the same style of architecture and the same venerable historic veneer. Until the beginning of the 1960s, Downtown retained its pure European stamp and old-timers doubtless can still remember that elegance. It was considered quite inappropriate for natives to wander around in Downtown in their gallabiyas and impossible for them to be allowed in this same traditional dress into restaurants such as Groppi's, À l'Américaine, and the Odéon, or even the Metro, Saint James, and Radio cinemas, and other places that required their patrons to wear, for men, suits, and, for the ladies, evening dresses. The stores all shut their doors on Sundays, and on the Catholic Christian holidays such as Christmas and New Year, Downtown was decorated all over, as though it were in a foreign capital. The glass frontages scintillated with holiday greetings in French and English, Christmas trees, and figures representing Father Christmas, and the restaurants and bars overflowed with foreigners and aristocrats who celebrated with drinking, singing, and dancing.

Downtown had always been full of small bars where people could take a few glasses and tasty dishes of *hors d'œuvres* in their free time and on weekends at a reasonable price. In the thirties and forties, some bars offered in addition to the drinks small entertainments by a Greek or Italian musician or a troupe of foreign Jewish women dancers. Up to the end of the 1960s, there were on Suleiman Basha alone almost ten small bars. Then came the 1970s, and the downtown area started gradually to lose its importance, the heart of Cairo moving to where the new élite lived, in El Mohandiseen and Medinet Nasr. An inexorable wave of religiosity swept Egyptian society and it became no longer socially acceptable to drink alcohol. Successive Egyptian governments bowed to the religious pressure (and perhaps attempted to outbid politically the opposition Islamist current) by restricting the sale of alcohol to the major hotels and restaurants and stopped issuing licenses for new bars; if the owner of a bar (usually a foreigner) died, the government would cancel the bar's license and require the heirs to change the nature of their business. On top of all this there were constant police raids on bars, during which the officers would frisk the patrons, inspect their identity cards, and sometimes accompany them to the police station for interrogation.

Thus it was that, as the 1980s dawned, there remained in the whole of Downtown only a few, scattered, small bars, whose owners had been able to hang on in the face of the rising tide of religion and government persecution. This they had been able to do by one of two methods—concealment or bribery. There was not one bar downtown that advertised its presence. Indeed, the very word "Bar" on the signs was changed to "Restaurant" or "Coffee Shop," and the owners of bars and wine stores deliberately painted the windows of their establishments a dark color so that what went on inside could not be seen, or would place in their display windows paper napkins or any other items that would not betray their actual business. It was no longer permitted for a customer to drink on the sidewalk in front of the bar or even in front of an open window that looked on to the street and stringent precautions had to be taken following the burning of a number of liquor stores at the hands of youths belonging to the Islamist movement.

At the same time, it was required of the few remaining bar owners that they pay large regular bribes to the plainclothes police officers to whose districts they belonged and to governorate officials in order for these to allow them to continue. Sometimes the sale of cheap locally produced alcohol would not realize them enough income to pay the fine, so that the bar owners found themselves obliged to find "other ways" of adding to their income. Some of them turned to facilitating prostitution by using fallen women to serve the alcohol, as was the case with the Cairo Bar in El Tawfikiya, and the Mido and the Pussycat on Emad el Din Street. Others turned to manufacturing alcohol in primitive laboratories instead of buying it, so as to increase profits. This happened at the Halegian Bar on Antikkhana Street and the Jamaica on Sherif Street. These disgusting industrially produced drinks led to a number of unfortunate accidents, the most celebrated of which befell a young artist who lost his sight after drinking bad brandy at the Halegian Bar. The public prosecutor's office ordered the bar closed but its owner was able to reopen later, using the usual methods.

Consequently, the small remaining downtown bars were no longer cheap, clean places for recreation as they had been before. Instead, they had turned into badly lit, poorly ventilated dens frequented mostly by hooligans and criminal types, though there were a few exceptions to this rule, such as Maxim's in the passage between Kasr el Nil and Suleiman Basha streets, and the Chez Nous, located beneath the Yacoubian Building.

The Chez Nous is a few steps below street level and thanks to the thick curtains the lighting is dim and shadowy even during the day. The large bar is to the left and the tables are benches of natural wood painted a dark color. The old lanterns of Viennese design, the works of art sculpted from wood or bronze and hung on the wall, the Latin-script writing on the paper tablecloths, and the huge beer glasses—all these things give the bar the appearance of an English "pub." In summer, as soon as you penetrate the Chez Nous, leaving behind you

Suleiman Basha with its noise, heat, and crowds and seat yourself to drink an ice-cold beer in the midst of the quiet, the powerful air conditioning, and the low, relaxing lighting, you feel as though you had gone into hiding from daily life in some way. This feeling of privacy is the great distinguishing feature of Chez Nous, which made its name basically as a meeting place for homosexuals (and which has made its way into more than one Western tourist guide under this rubric).

The owner of the bar is called Aziz. He is nicknamed "the Englishman" (because, with his white complexion, yellow hair, and blue eyes, he resembles one) and he is a victim of that same condition. They say he took up with the old Greek who used to own the bar and that the latter fell in love with him and made him a present of the establishment before his death. They whisper too that he organizes outrageous parties at which he introduces homosexuals to Arab tourists and that homosexual prostitution brings him in huge profits with which he pays the bribes that have made his place into a safe haven from the annoying attentions of the security forces. He is blessed with a strong presence and *savoir-faire* and under his supervision and care homosexuals meet at Chez Nous and form friendships there, released from the social pressures that prevent them from advertising their tendencies.

Places where homosexuals meet are like hashish cafés and gambling dens in that their patrons belong to all social levels and are of varying ages. You find among them skilled workers and professionals, young people and old, all united by their homosexuality. By the same token, homosexuals, like burglars, pickpockets, and all other groups outside the laws and norms of society, have created for themselves a special language that enables them to understand one another when among strangers. Thus they call a passive homosexual a "kudyana" and give him a girl's name by which he is known among them, such as Souad, Angie, Fatma, and so on. They call an active homosexual a "barghal," and if he is ignorant and simple, they call him a "rough barghal." They call male-to-male sex a "hook-up." They make themselves known to one another and hold secret conversations by means of hand movements. Thus if one of them takes the other's hand and strokes his wrist with his finger while shaking it, that means that he desires him and if a homosexual brings two fingers together and moves them while talking to someone, this means that he is inviting his interlocutor to have sex, and if he points to his heart with one finger, it means that his lover has sole possession of his heart, and so on.

Just as Aziz the Englishman looks out for the comfort and good cheer of the Chez Nous patrons, so by the same token he permits them no indecent behavior. As the night and the patrons' indulgence in drink progress, their voices grow louder, rise in pitch, and interrupt one another, for the desire to talk takes possession of them, as happens in all bars. The drunkards at Chez Nous, however, fall prey to a combination of lust and intoxication, exchanging endearments and dirty jokes, and one of them will sometimes stretch out his fingers to caress his friend's body—at which point, Aziz the Englishman intervenes at once, using every means to re-impose order, starting with a polite whisper and ending with a threat to throw the delinquent customer out of the bar. Often the Englishman gets so excited that his face turns red while he berates the homosexual whose lust has been aroused saying, "Listen. As long as you're at my place, behave yourself. If you fancy your friend that much, get up and go off with him, but don't you lay a hand on him in this bar!"

The Englishman's sternness here does not stem from any concern for morality of course but from calculations of profit and loss, since plainclothes officers often visit the bar. True, they satisfy themselves with a quick glance from a distance and don't disturb the patrons at all (thanks to the large bribes they receive) but if they were to witness any scandalous act there they would make a huge fuss, since that would be their opportunity to blackmail the Englishman into paying even more.

A little before midnight, the door of the bar opened and Hatim Rasheed appeared with a dark-complexioned young man in his twenties wearing inexpensive clothes, his hair cropped like a soldier. The people in the bar were drunk, shouting and singing loudly. All the same as soon as Hatim entered their racket diminished and they took to observing him with curiosity and a certain awe. They knew that he was a kudyana but a forbidding natural reserve prevented them from acting familiarly with him and even the most impudent and obscene of the customers could do no other than treat him with respect.

There were a number of reasons for this. Hatim Rasheed is a well-known journalist and editor-in-chief of the newspaper *Le Caire*, which comes out in Cairo in French. He is an aristocrat of ancient lineage whose mother was French and whose father was Dr. Hassan Rasheed, the famous jurist and dean of the College of Law in the 1950s. In addition, Hatim Rasheed is a conservative homosexual, if that is the right expression: he does not sacrifice his dignity, put powder on his face, or stoop to using provocative ways as do many kudyanas. In appearance and behavior he always chooses a skilful compromise between elegance and femininity. Tonight for instance he is wearing a dark wine-red suit and has knotted around his slender neck a yellow scarf, most of which he has tucked under his pink, natural-silk shirt, the two ends of the latter's broad collar flopping over the front of his jacket. With his smart clothes, svelte figure, and fine French features, he would look like a scintillating movie star were it not for the wrinkles that his riotous life has left on his face and that miserable, unpleasant, mysterious, gloomy look that always haunts the faces of homosexuals.

Aziz the Englishman went toward him to welcome him and Hatim shook his hand affectionately, gesturing gracefully toward his young friend and saying, "My friend Abd Rabbuh, who's doing his military service in Central Security."

"Pleased to meet you," said Aziz, smiling and looking the strong, muscular young man over. Then he led his two guests to a quiet table at the end of the bar and took their orders—gin and tonic for Hatim, an imported beer for Abd Rabbuh, and some hot *hors d'œuvres*. Gradually, the customers lost interest in them and resumed their talk and raucous laughter.

The two friends appeared to be engrossed in a long and wearisome argument, Hatim speaking in a low voice and looking at his friend as though trying to convince him of something, Abd Rabbuh listening unmoved and then replying vehemently. Hatim would remain silent for a moment, his head bowed, then resume the attempt. The conversation went on this way for almost half an hour, during which the two companions drank two bottles of beer and three glasses of gin, and at the end of which Hatim leant his back once more against the back of the seat and directed a penetrating glance at Abduh.

"That's your last word?"

Abduh replied in a loud voice, the alcohol having gone quickly to his head, "Yes!"

"Abduh, come with me tonight and we'll work things out in the morning."

"No."

"Please, Abduh."

"No."

"Very well. Can we work things out quietly? None of that quick temper of yours!" whispered Hatim winningly, touching with his fingers his friend's huge hand as it lay on the table. This insistence seemed to exasperate Abduh who let out his breath in annoyance and said, "I told you I can't stay with you tonight. I was late three times last week because of you. The officer will refer me for disciplining."

"Don't worry! I've found someone who can put in a good word for you with the officer."

"Ouff!" screamed Abduh with annoyance, pushing the beer glass with his hand so that it fell over with a ringing crash. Then he got up, directed an angry look at Hatim, and rushed to the exit. Hatim pulled some notes out of his wallet, threw them on the table, and hurried after his friend. For a few moments, silence reigned in the bar. Then the drunken comments rang out:

"A barghal with attitude, me boys!"

"Pity the one who loves and can't get no satisfaction!"

"What to do, Honey, now you done used up all my money?"

The men laughed uproariously and burst enthusiastically and with resonant voices into a round of indecent songs, so that Aziz the Englishman was obliged to intervene to restore order.

Like most Egyptians from the countryside, Muhammad el Sayed, cook's assistant at the Automobile Club, had suffered from bilharzia, which he contracted early on in life and which had led to inflammation and failure of the liver by the time he reached fifty. Busayna, his eldest daughter, remembers well the day in Ramadan when, after the family had eaten its breakfast meal in their small apartment with its two rooms and a latrine on the roof of the Yacoubian Building and her father had gone to perform the evening prayer, they suddenly heard the sound of something heavy falling to the ground. Busayna remembers too her mother's agonized scream, "Go help your father!" They all ran to him—Busayna, Sawsan, Fatin, and little Mustafa. Their father was lying on the bed in his white gallabiya, his body completely still and his face a dull blue. Once they had called the ambulance and the raw young doctor had made a quick examination and announced the sad news, the girls let out piercing screams and their mother started slapping hard at her face, keeping it up till she fell to the floor.

At the time Busayna was studying for a commercial diploma and had dreams for the future that it would never have occurred to her might not come true: she was going to graduate and marry her sweetheart Taha el Shazli after he graduated from the Police College, and they would live in a nice spacious apartment a long way from the Yacoubian roof, and they would have just one boy and one girl so that they could raise them properly. They had everything worked out but her father had died suddenly and with the passing of the mourning period the family found itself destitute. The pension was meager and did not cover the costs of schooling, food, clothes, and rent. Her mother soon changed. She always wore black, her body withered and dried out, and her face took on that stern, masculine, prickly look that poor widows have. Little by little she grew bad-tempered and took to quarreling all the time with the girls; even little Mustafa wasn't spared her beatings and abuse. After each scene she would abandon herself to a long bout of crying. She stopped talking about the departed with the great affection she had shown in the early days and instead starting talking about him in a bitter and disappointed way, as though he had let her down and deliberately left her in this mess. She started disappearing two or three days a week, leaving in the morning and returning at the end of the day exhausted, silent, and distracted, carrying bags of cooked food all mixed up together (rice and vegetables and little bits of meat or chicken) which she would heat and give them to eat.

The day Busayna passed her exams and got her diploma her mother waited until night had fallen and the rest of the family was asleep and took her out onto the roof. It was a hot summer night and men were smoking goza and chatting the evening away while a few women were sitting in the open air to escape the heat of their cramped iron rooms. The mother greeted them and pulled Busayna by her hand to a distant part of the roof, where they stood next to the wall. Busayna can still recall the sight of the cars and the lights of Suleiman Basha as they appeared that night from the roof, along with her mother's frowning face, her stern, penetrating looks, and her harsh, strange voice as she spoke to her of the burden the departed had left her with to endure on her own, and informed her that she was working in the house of some good-hearted people in Zamalek but had kept it a secret so that it wouldn't affect Busayna's or her sisters' marriage prospects (when people found out that their mother was working as a maid). The mother asked Busayna to look for a job for herself, starting the next day. Busayna did not reply but looked at her mother for a little, overwhelmed by tenderness. Then she bent down toward her and hugged her. It occurred to her as she kissed her that her face had gotten dry and coarse and that a new, strange smell came off her body—the smell of sweat mixed with dust that maids give off.

The next day Busayna put everything she had in her into finding a job and in one year she went through lots—secretary in a lawyer's office, assistant to a women's hairdresser, trainee nurse at a dentist's. Every job she left for the same reason and after going through the same rigmarole—the warm welcome from the boss accompanied by enormous, burning interest, followed by the little kindnesses and the presents and small gifts of money, with the hints that there was more where that came from, all to be met from her side with a refusal well coated in politeness (so that she wouldn't lose the job). However, the boss would keep at it till the business reached its logical conclusion, that final scene that she hated and feared and that always came about when the older man would insist on kissing her by force in the empty office, or press up against her, or start opening his fly to confront her with some "facts on the ground." Then she would push him away and threaten to scream and make a scene, at which point he would switch and show his vengeful face by throwing her out after mocking her by calling her "Khadra el Shareefa." Or sometimes he would pretend that he was just testing her morals and assure her that he loved her like his own daughter, in which case he would wait for the right time (after any danger of scandal had passed) and throw her out on any other excuse.

During that year Busayna learned a lot. She discovered for example that her beautiful and provocative body, her wide, dark-brown eyes and full lips, her voluptuous breasts and tremulous, rounded backside with its soft buttocks, all had an important role to play in her dealings with people. It became clear to her that all men, however respectable in appearance and however elevated their position in society, were utter weaklings in front of a beautiful woman. This drove her to try out some wicked but entertaining tests. Thus, if she met a respectable old man whom she thought it would be fun to test, she would put on a girlish voice and bend over and stick out her voluptuous breasts, then immediately enjoy the sight of the sober-sided gentleman going soft and trembly, his eyes clouding over with desire. The way men panted after her gave her a gloating pleasure similar to that of revenge. It also became clear to her during that year that her mother had changed completely for whenever Busayna left a job because of the men's importunities, her mother would greet the news with a silence akin to exasperation and on one occasion, after it had happened several times, she told Busayna as she got up to leave the room, "Your brother and sisters need every penny you earn. A clever girl can look after herself and keep her job." This sentence saddened and puzzled Busayna, who asked herself, "How can I look after myself when faced with a boss who opens his fly?"

She remained in the same state of puzzlement for many long weeks, until Fifi, the daughter of Sabir the laundryman, who was a neighbor of theirs on the roof, appeared. She had heard that Busayna was looking for work and had come to tell her about a job as a sales-girl at the Shanan clothing store. When Busayna told her about her problem with earlier bosses, Fifi let out a great sigh, struck her on her chest, and shouted in her face in disbelief, "Don't be a fool, girl!" Fifi explained to her that more than ninety percent of bosses did that with the girls who worked for them and that any girl who refused was thrown out and a hundred other girls who didn't object could be found to take her place. When Busayna started to object, Fifi asked her sarcastically, "So Your Ladyship has an MBA from the American University? Why, the beggars in the street have commercial diplomas the same as you!"

Fifi explained to her that going along with the boss "up to a point" was just being smart and that the world was one thing and what she saw in Egyptian movies was another. She explained to her that she knew lots of girls who had worked for years at the Shanan store and given Mr. Talal, the owner of the store, what he wanted "up to a point" and were now happily married with kids, homes, and husbands who loved them lots. "But why go so far afield?" Fifi asked, citing herself as an example. She had worked in the store for two years and her salary was a hundred pounds but she earned at least three times that much by "being smart," not to mention the presents. And all the same, she had been able to look after herself, she was a virgin, and she'd scratch out the eyes of anyone who said anything against her reputation. There were a hundred men who wanted to marry her, especially now that she was earning and putting her money into saving co-ops and setting money aside to pay for her trousseau.

The next day Busayna went with Fifi to Mr. Talal at the store. He turned out to be over forty, fair-complexioned, blue-eyed, balding, and stout. He was snub-nosed and had a huge black moustache that hung down on either side of his mouth. Mr. Talal was not at all handsome, and Busayna found out that he was the only son, among a bunch of girls, of Hagg Shanan, a Syrian, who had come from Syria during the Union and settled in Egypt and opened this store. Once he started getting on, he had handed his business over to his only son. She learned too that he was married and that his wife was Egyptian and pretty and had borne him two sons, though despite all that his predations on women never stopped. Talal shook Busayna's hand (giving it a squeeze) and never raised his eyes from her chest and body while he spoke. After a few minutes, she started her new job.

In just a few weeks, Fifi had taught her all she had to do: how she had to take care of her appearance, paint her fingernails and her toenails, open the neck of her dress a little, and take her dresses in a bit at the waist to show off her backside. It was her job to open the store in the morning and mop it out along with her colleagues, then set her clothes straight and stand at the door (a way of attracting customers familiar to all the clothing stores). When she had a customer, she had to talk to him nicely, comply with his requests, and persuade him to buy as much as possible (she got a half of one percent of the value of all sales). Naturally, she had to put up with the customers' flirting, however obnoxious.

That was the job. As for "the other thing," Mr. Talal started in on it the third day after she came. It was the time of the afternoon prayer and the store was empty of customers. Talal asked her to go with him to the storeroom so that he could explain to her the different items they had in stock. Busayna followed him without a word, noting the shadow of an ironic smile on the faces of Fifi and the other girls.

The storeroom consisted of a large apartment on the ground floor in the building next to the À l'Américaine café on Suleiman Basha. Talal entered and locked the door from the inside. She looked about her. The place was damp and badly lit and ventilated and was stacked to the ceiling with boxes. She knew what was coming and had readied herself on the way to the storeroom, repeating to herself in her head her mother's words, "Your brother and sisters need every penny you earn. A clever girl can look after herself and keep her job." When Mr. Talal came close to her, she was struck by strong and conflicting feelings—determination to make the best of the opportunity and the fear which despite everything still wracked her and made her fight for breath and feel as though she was about to be sick. There was also a sneaking, covert curiosity that urged her to find out what Mr. Talal would do to her. Would he woo her and tell her, "I love you," for example, or try to kiss her right away? She found out quickly enough because Talal pounced on her from behind, flung his arms around her hard enough to hurt her and started rubbing up against her and playing with her body without uttering a single word. He was violent and in a hurry to get his pleasure and the whole business was over in about two minutes. Her dress was soiled and he whispered to her, panting, "The bathroom's at the end of the corridor on the right."

As she washed her dress in the water, she thought to herself that the whole thing was easier than she'd imagined, like some man rubbing up against her in the bus (something that happened a lot) and she remembered what Fifi had told her to do after the encounter. She went back to Talal and said to him in a voice she made as smooth and seductive as she could, "I need twenty pounds from you, sir." Talal looked at her for a moment, then quickly thrust his hand into his pocket as though he had been expecting the request and said in an ordinary voice as he took out a folded banknote, "Nah. Ten's enough. Come back to the store after me as soon as your dress is dry." Then he went out, closing the door behind him.

Ten pounds a time, and Mr. Talal would ask for her twice, sometimes three times a week, and Fifi had taught her how from time to time to show her liking for a dress in the shop and keep on at Talal until he made her a present of it. She started making money and wearing nice clothes and her mother was pleased with her and was comforted by the money that she took from her and tucked into the front of her dress, uttering warm blessings for her after doing so. Listening to these, Busayna was overwhelmed with a mysterious, malign desire to start giving her mother clear hints about her relationship with Talal, but her mother would ignore any such messages. Busayna would then go to such lengths with her hints that the mother's refusal to acknowledge them became obvious and extremely fragile, at which point Busayna would feel some relief, as though she had snatched away her mother's mask of false innocence and confirmed her complicity in the crime.

As time passed her rendezvous with Talal in the storeroom had an impact on her that she would never have imagined. She found herself no longer able to perform the morning prayer (the only one of the required prayers that she had performed) because inwardly she was ashamed to face "Our Lord," because she felt herself unclean, however much she performed the ablutions. She started having nightmares and would start up from her sleep terrified. She would go for days depressed and melancholy and one day when she went with her mother to visit the tomb of El Hussein, no sooner had she entered the sanctuary and found herself surrounded by the incense and lights and felt that deeply-rooted hidden presence that fills the heart than she burst into a long, unexpected, bout of weeping.

On the other hand since retreat was not an option and she could not stand her feelings of sin, she started to resist the latter fiercely. She took to thinking of her mother's face as she told her that she was working as a servant in people's houses. She would repeat to herself what Fifi had said about the world and how it worked and often she would contemplate the shop's rich, chic, women customers and ask herself with spiteful passion, "I wonder how many times that woman surrendered her body to get to where she is now?"

This violent resistance to her feelings of guilt left a legacy of bitterness and cruelty. She stopped trusting people or making excuses for them. She would often think (and then seek forgiveness) that God had wanted her to fall. If He had wanted otherwise, He would have created her a rich woman or delayed her father's death a few years (and what could have been easier for Him?). Little by little, her resentment extended to include her sweetheart Taha himself. A strange feeling that she was stronger than he was by far would creep over her—a feeling that she was mature and understood the world, while he was just a dreamy, naïve boy. She started to get annoyed at his optimism about the future and speak sharply to him, mocking him by saying, "You think you're Abd el Halim Hafez? The poor, hard-working boy whose dreams will come true if he struggles?"

At first, Taha didn't understand the reason for this bitterness. Then her sarcasm at his expense started to provoke him and they would quarrel, and when he asked her once to stop working for Talal because he had a bad reputation, she looked at him challengingly and said, "At your service, sir. Give me the two hundred and fifty pounds that I earn from Talal and you'll have the right to stop me showing my face to anyone but you." He stared at her for a moment as though he did not understand and then his anger erupted and he shoved her on the shoulder. She screamed insults at him and threw at him a silver outfit he'd bought for her. In the depths of her heart, she craved to rip her relationship with him to pieces so that she might be freed of that painful feeling of sin that tortured her as soon as she set eyes on him, yet it was not in her power to leave him completely. She loved him and they had a long history full of beautiful moments. The instant she saw him sad or anxious, she would forget everything and envelop him in genuine, overflowing tenderness as though she was his mother. However bad the quarrels between them got, she would make up with him and go back to him, and their affair was not without rare and wonderful times. Very soon, however, the gloom would return.

Busayna spent the whole day blaming herself for her cruelty to him that morning when he had been in need of a word of encouragement from her as he set off for a test that she knew he had been waiting for for many years. How cruel that had been of her! What would it have hurt her to encourage him with a word and a smile? If only she had spent a little time with him! After work she found herself anxious to meet him, so she went to Tawfikiya Square and sat waiting for him on the wall of the flowerbed where they usually met each evening. Night had fallen and the square was crowded with passersby and vendors; sitting on her own she was subjected to a lot of harassment but she kept waiting for him for almost half an hour. When he didn't come, she thought he must be angry with her because she had put him off that morning, so she got up and climbed the stairs to his room on the roof. The door was open and Taha's mother was sitting there alone, anxiety showing on her aged face. The mother hugged her and kissed her, then sat her down next to her on the bench and said, "I'm very scared, Busayna. Taha left for the exam in the morning and still hasn't come back. Pray God he's all right!"

Were it not for his advanced age and the years of hardship that have left their traces on his countenance, Hagg Muhammad Azzam would look like a movie star or a crowned head, with his towering height and imperturbable gravitas, his elegance and his wealth, his face rosy with overflowing good health and his complexion all polished and shiny thanks to the skill of the experts at La Gaité Beauty Center in El Mohandiseen where he goes once a week. He owns more than a hundred suits of the most luxurious kind and wears a different one every day, with a showy necktie and elegant imported shoes.

Each day, in the middle of the morning, Hagg Azzam's red Mercedes rolls down Suleiman Basha from the direction of the À l'Américaine with him seated in the back absorbed in telling the small amber prayer beads that never leave his hand. His day starts with an inspection of his properties—two large clothing stores, one of them opposite the À l'Américaine, the other on the ground floor of the Yacoubian Building where his office is situated; two automobile showrooms; and a number of spare parts shops in Marouf Street, not to mention a great deal of real estate in the downtown area and many other buildings that are under construction, soon to rise in the form of towering skyscrapers bearing the name Azzam

Contractors. The car proceeds to stop in front of each establishment and the employees gather round it to offer the Hagg warm greetings, which he returns with a wave of his hand so restrained and insignificant that you might not notice it. The head employee or the most senior among them immediately approaches the car window, bends toward the Hagg, and briefs him on the work situation or seeks his advice on some matter. Hagg Azzam listens carefully with his head lowered, his thick eyebrows knotted, his lips pursed, then trains his narrow, gray foxy eyes (always slightly red from the effects of hashish) on the distance, as though he were watching something on the horizon. Finally he speaks, his voice deep, its intonation decisive, the words few and far between. He cannot abide chatter or disputatiousness.

Some attribute his love of silence to his application (with his strictly observant piety) of the noble hadith that says, "If one of you speaks let him be brief, or let him stay silent"—though at the same time, with his vast wealth and extraordinary influence, he does not in fact need to talk much because his word is generally final and has to be obeyed. To this should be added his wide experience of life that enables him to grasp things at a glance, for the aging millionaire, who is past sixty, started out thirty years ago as a mere migrant worker who left Sohag governorate for Cairo looking for work, and the older people on Suleiman Basha remember him sitting on the ground in the passage behind the À l'Américaine in a gallabiya, vest, and turban with a small wooden box in front of him—for that is where he started, shining shoes. He worked for a time as an office servant in the Babik office supplies store, then disappeared for more than twenty years, suddenly to reappear having made a lot of money. Hagg Azzam says that he was working in the Gulf but the people in the street do not believe that and whisper that he was sentenced and imprisoned for dealing in drugs, which some insist he continues to do to this day, citing as evidence his exorbitant wealth, which is out of all proportion to the volume of the sales in his stores and the profits of his companies, indicating that his commercial activities are a mere front for money laundering.

Whatever the accuracy of these rumors, Hagg Azzam has become the unrivalled 'big man' of Suleiman Basha and people seek him out to get their business done and settle their differences, while his influence has been consolidated recently by his joining the Patriotic Party and by his youngest son Hamdi subsequently joining the judiciary as a public prosecutor. Hagg Azzam has an overwhelming urge to buy property and shops in the downtown district specifically, as though to stress his new situation in the area that once witnessed him as a poor down-and-out.

It was about two years ago that Hagg Azzam woke to perform the dawn prayer, as was his custom, and found his nightwear wet. He was disturbed and it occurred to him that he might be sick, but when he went into the bathroom to wash, he ascertained that the cause of the wetness was a sexual urge and he remembered the distorted image of a naked, distant woman that he had seen in his dreams. This strange phenomenon with an old man like himself astonished him. He forgot about it during the busy day but it happened again several times thereafter, so that he had to bathe daily before the dawn prayer to cleanse himself of the defilement. Nor did things end there, for he caught himself several times stealing glances at the bodies of the women working for him in the store and some of them, instinctively sensing his lust, started to walk with a deliberately provocative gait and talk coquettishly in front of him to seduce him, so that several times he was forced to scold them.

These sudden importunate sexual urges disturbed Hagg Azzam greatly, firstly because they were inappropriate to his age and secondly because he had kept to the strait and narrow all his life and believed that his uprightness and avoidance of anything that might make God angry was the main reason for all the success he had achieved—for he never drank alcohol. (As for the hashish that he smoked, many religious experts had assured him that it was merely "reprehensible" and neither created uncleanness nor was absolutely prohibited. In addition it neither took away the mental faculties nor drove man to commit indecencies or crimes as did alcohol; on the contrary, hashish calmed a man's nerves, brought him greater equipoise, and sharpened his mind.) Likewise, the Hagg had never committed fornication in his entire life, immunizing himself, like most Sa'idis, by marrying early; also over the course of his long life he had witnessed wealthy men surrender to their lusts and lose vast fortunes.

The Hagg confided his problem to certain older friends of his and they assured him that what was happening was an ephemeral phenomenon that would soon disappear forever. "It's just an excess of good health," said his friend Hagg Kamil the cement trader, laughing. But the urges continued as the days passed and intensified until they became a heavy burden on his nerves and, even worse, were the cause of a number of tiffs with Hagga Salha, his wife, who was a few years younger than him but was caught unprepared by this sudden blossoming of youthfulness and then got upset because she was unable to satisfy him. More than once she rebuked him and told him that their children were grown men and that as two older spouses they ought to adorn themselves with an appropriate sedateness.

Nothing was left to Hagg Azzam but to take the matter to Sheikh El Samman, the celebrated man of religion and president of the Islamic Charitable Association whom Azzam considers his spiritual leader and guide in all matters pertaining to this world and the next, to the degree that he will not reach a firm decision on any subject that concerns him in his work or his life without having recourse to him. He puts at his disposal thousands of pounds, to be spent, with his knowledge, on charitable works, not to mention the valuable gifts that he gives him every time a good business deal has gone through as a result of his prayers and blessings.

After the Friday prayer and the weekly class in religion that Sheikh El Samman delivers at the Salam Mosque in Medinet Nasr, Hagg Azzam requested a private interview with the sheikh and talked to him about his problem. The sheikh listened attentively, was silent for a while, then said with a vehemence that was not far from anger, "Glory be, Hagg! Why, my brother, make things difficult for yourself when God has made them easy for you? Why open the door for Satan, so that you can fall into error? You have to protect yourself, as God commanded. God has made marriage to more than one wife lawful for you so long as you behave with justice. Put your trust in God and make haste to do what is right before you fall into what is wrong!"

"I'm an old man. I'm afraid of what people might say if I married."

"If I didn't know your righteousness and godfearingness, I would think badly of you. Which is worthier of your fear, man? What people say, or the anger of the Merciful, Glorious and Magnificent? Would you make forbidden what God has made lawful? You are potent, your health is excellent, and you find in yourself a desire for women. Marry and treat both your wives equally. God loves you to make lawful use of what He has permitted."

Hagg Azzam hesitated for a long while (or made a show of doing so) but Sheikh El Samman kept on at him until he convinced him. He even (and for this he was to be thanked) undertook to convince his three sons, Fawzi, Qadri, and Hamdi (the public prosecutor). The last two received the news of their father's wish to get married with astonishment but accepted it anyway. Fawzi, the elder son and his father's right hand at work, seemed not to approve, though he did not make his reason for objecting explicit. In the end, he said grudgingly, "If the Hagg has to marry, then it's up to us to make sure he chooses well, so he doesn't fall into the hands of some bitch who will make his life hell."

The principle was established, then, and it remained to mount a search for a suitable wife. Hagg Azzam commissioned his most trusted friends to look for a nice girl and during the next few months saw many candidates but with his broad experience refused any in whose conduct he found anything to object to. This one was outstandingly lovely but had her face uncovered, was pert, and he could not entrust her with his honor; that one was young and spoiled and would exhaust him with her demands; and the one after was greedy and loved money. Thus, the Hagg refused all candidates until he met Souad Gaber, a salesclerk in the Hannaux department store in Alexandria. She was divorced and had one son and as soon as the Hagg saw her she beguiled his heart—a light-skinned woman, full-bodied, beautiful, who covered her hair, which was black and smooth and flowing, the tresses peeking out from beneath her headscarf. The eyes were black, wide, and bewitching, the lips plump and sensual, and she was clean and her attention to the minutiae of her body was outstanding as is usually the case with the women of Alexandria. Her finger and toenails were clipped and the tips were cleaned, though they were not painted (so that the varnish would not form an impediment to the water she used for her ritual ablutions). Her hands were soft, tender-skinned, and rubbed with cream. Even her heels were extremely clean, smooth, firm, and free of any cracking, and were suffused with a delicate redness as a result of being polished with pumice.

Souad left a delicate, fascinating impression on the Hagg's heart. What pleased him specially was the meekness that poverty and a hard life had left her with. He considered that her history was in no way blameworthy: she had married a house painter, who had left her a son and then abandoned her and gone off to Iraq, where nothing more was heard from him; the court had granted her a divorce so that her situation should not lead to social problems.

The Hagg sent people secretly to ask about her at her work and home and everyone praised her for her morals. Then he performed the prayer for guidance in choice and Souad Gaber appeared to him in a dream in all her beauty (but decently dressed and not naked and vulgar like the women of whom he usually dreamed). As a result, Hagg Azzam put his trust in God and visited Souad's family in Sidi Bishr, sat down with Rayyis Hamidu, her elder brother (who worked as a waiter in a café in El Manshiya), and agreed with him on everything. Hagg Azzam, who was, as usual when conducting a business transaction, clear and frank and not disposed to bargain, married Souad Gaber on the following conditions:

1   That Souad come and live with him in Cairo and leave her small son Tamir with her mother in Alexandria, it being understood that she could go and visit him "when convenient."

2   That he should buy her jewelry to a value of ten thousand pounds as an engagement present and that he should pay a bride price of twenty thousand pounds, it being understood that the amount to be paid in the case of an eventual divorce should not exceed five thousand pounds.

3   That the marriage should remain a secret and that it be clearly understood that in the case of Hagga Salha, his wife, finding out about his new marriage, he would be compelled to divorce Souad forthwith.

4   That, while the marriage was to be conducted according to the norms set by God and His Prophet, he had no desire whatsoever for offspring.

Hagg Azzam stressed this last condition, making it extremely clear to Rayyis Hamidu that neither his age nor his circumstances permitted him to be father to a child at this time and that if Souad got pregnant, the agreement would be considered abrogated forthwith.

"What's wrong?"

The two of them were on the bed, Souad in her blue nightgown that revealed her full, trembling breasts, her thighs, and her amazingly white arms, Hagg Azzam stretched out beside her on his back wearing his white gallabiya. This was their hour—every day after the Hagg had performed the afternoon prayer in his office and gone up to her in the luxury apartment that he had bought her on the seventh floor of the building to take his lunch, after which he would sleep with her till before the last prayer and then leave her until the following day. This was the only regime that allowed him to see her without disturbing his family life.

Today, however, he was, unlike his usual self, exhausted and anxious. He was thinking about something that had kept him distracted all day long but now he was tired of thinking and had a headache and nausea from the several hand-rolled cigarettes he had smoked after eating and he wished Souad would leave him to sleep for a little. She, however, stretched out her hands, took his head between their soft palms with their sweetly perfumed scent, looked at him for a while with her wide, black eyes, and whispered, "What's wrong, my dear?"

The Hagg smiled and mumbled, "Lots of problems at work."

"Praise God you've got your health. That's the most important thing."

"Praise God."

"I swear to Almighty God, the world isn't worth a second's worry!"

"You're right."

"Tell me what's bothering you, Hagg."

"As though you don't have enough problems of your own!"

"Go on with you! Are my problems more important than yours?"

The Hagg smiled and looked at her gratefully. Then he moved closer, planted a kiss on her cheek, pulled his head back a little, and said in a serious voice, "God willing, I intend to put myself forward for the People's Assembly."

"The People's Assembly?"

"Yes."

She was taken aback for a moment because it was so unexpected but she soon pulled herself together and wreathed her face in a happy smile, saying gaily, "What a wonderful day, Hagg! Should I whoop for joy or what?"

"Let's just hope that things go well and I get elected."

"God willing."

"You know, Souad, if I get into the Assembly . . . I can do business worth millions."

"Of course you'll get in. Could they find anyone better than you?"

Then she puckered up her lips as though talking down to a child and said to him (using the words one would to a little girl), "But I'm scared, sweetie, that when you appear on television and everyone sees you looking so cute, they'll go steal you away from me!"

The Hagg burst into laughter and she moved up close so he could feel the warmth of her excited body. Then she reached over with her hand in an unhurried, practiced, long-lasting caress that finally yielded its fruits, and let out a ribald laugh when she saw that in his enthusiasm and haste, he had got his head stuck in the neck of his gallabiya.

It was just like that when you watch a film—you get engrossed in it and you react to it, but in the end the lights go back on, you return to reality, you leave the cinema, and the cold air of the street, crowded with cars and passersby, strikes you on the face; everything returns to its normal size and you think of everything that happened as just a movie, just a lot of acting.

That's how Taha el Shazli recalls the events of the day of the character interview: the long corridor of luxurious red carpet, the huge spacious room with its lofty ceiling, the large desk raised enough above floor level to make it seem like the dais in a courtroom, the low leather seat on which he sat, the three generals with their huge flabby bodies, white suits, shiny brass buttons, signs of rank, and glittering decorations on their chests and shoulders, and the presiding general, who welcomed him with a precisely measured, disciplined smile and then nodded to the committee member on his right. The latter propped his arms on the desk, stuck his bald head forward, and started asking him questions, the other two watching him closely as though weighing every word he spoke and observing every expression that appeared on his face. The questions were what he'd expected, his officer friends having assured him that the character interview questions were always the same and well-known, the whole test being no more than a formality carried out for appearances' sake, either to exclude radical elements (based on the National Security Service reports) or to confirm the acceptance of those blessed with influential friends. Taha had memorized the expected questions and their model answers and proceeded steadily and confidently to give his answers before the committee. He said that he had obtained high enough marks to qualify for one of the good colleges but preferred the Police College so that he could serve his country from his position as a police officer. He stressed that the job of the police was not simply to maintain order, as many thought, but social and humanitarian (giving examples of what he meant). Next he spoke about preventive security, in terms of definition and methods, approval appearing clearly on the examiners' faces and the presiding general even nodding his head twice in confirmation of Taha's answer. The former then spoke for the first time and asked Taha what he would do if he went to arrest a criminal and found him to be one of his childhood friends. Taha was expecting the question and had prepared the reply but he made a show of thinking a bit to increase the impact of his answer on the examiners. Then he said, "Sir, duty knows nothing of friends or relatives. A policeman is like a soldier in battle—he must carry out his duty irrespective of all other considerations, for the sake of God and his country."

The presiding general smiled and nodded with frank admiration and the silence that comes before the end reigned. Taha expected that the order to dismiss would be given but the presiding general suddenly looked hard at the papers as though he had just discovered something. He raised the sheet of paper a little to make sure of what he had read, then asked Taha, avoiding his eyes, "Your father—what's his profession, Taha?"

"Civil servant, sir."

(This is what he had written on the application form, after paying the Community Liaison Officer a bribe of a hundred pounds to sign off on it.) The general searched through the papers again and said, "Civil servant, or property guard?"

Taha said nothing for a moment. Then he said in a low voice, "My father is a property guard, sir."

The presiding general smiled and looked embarrassed. Then he bent over the papers, carefully wrote something on them, raised his head with the same smile, and said, "Thanks, son. Dismissed."

His mother sighed and quoted the Qur'anic verse, "*It may happen that you will hate a thing which is better for you.*"

Busayna cried out vehemently, "What's so special about being a police officer? Police officers are as common as dirt. How happy I would have been to see your officer's uniform, when you were earning pennies!"

Taha had spend the day roaming the streets till he was exhausted and then come home to the roof and sat with his head bowed on the bench, the suit that he had put on that morning stripped of its glamour, baggy now and looking cheap and wretched. His mother tried to cheer him up.

"Son, you're making things too complicated. There are lots of other good colleges apart from the police."

Taha remained bowed and silent. It seemed it was beyond his mother's words to deal with the matter and she disappeared into the kitchen, leaving him with Busayna, who moved over to sit next to him on the bench. She drew close to him and whispered, "Please don't upset yourself, Taha."

Her voice set him off and he cried out bitterly, "I'm upset because of all my wasted effort. If they'd set a particular profession for the father from the start, I would have known. They should have said 'No children of doorkeepers.' And what they did is against the law, too. I asked a lawyer and he told me that if I brought a case against them, I'd win."

"We don't want a court case or anything of that sort. Know what I think? With the grades you've got, you should enter the best college in the university, graduate with top marks, go off to an Arab country and earn some money, then come back here and live like a king."

Taha looked at her for a while, then hung his head again. She went on, "Look, Taha. I know I'm a year younger than you but I've worked and work has taught me a few things. This country doesn't belong to us, Taha. It belongs to the people who have money. If you'd had twenty thousand pounds and used them to bribe someone, do you think any one would have asked about your father's job? Make money, Taha, and you'll get everything but if you stay poor they'll walk all over you."

"I can't let them get away with it. I must make a complaint."

Busayna laughed bitterly. "Complain about who and to who? Do as I say and no more useless ideas. Work hard, get your degree, and don't come back here till you're rich. And if you never come back, better still."

"So you think I should go to one of the Arab countries?"

"Certainly."

"Will you come with me?"

The question took her by surprise and she mumbled, avoiding his eyes, "God willing." But he said sadly, "You've changed toward me, Busayna. I know it."

Busayna could see another quarrel coming, so she said with a sigh, "You're tired out now. Go get some sleep and we'll talk tomorrow."

She left but he didn't sleep. He stayed awake for a long while thinking, recalling a hundred times the face of the presiding general as he asked him slowly, as though reveling in his humiliation, "Your father's a property guard, son?" "Property guard?"—an unfamiliar expression, one that he'd given no thought to and that he'd never expected. An expression that was his whole life. He had lived it for long years, suffered its oppression, resisted it with all his might, and tried to rid himself of it. He had struggled so that he might escape through the opening provided by the Police College into a respectable, decent life, but that expression—"property guard"—was waiting for him at the end of the exhausting race, to ruin everything at the final moment. Why hadn't they told him at the beginning? Why had the general left it to the end and shown how pleased he was with his answers to the questions, then directed his final thrust at him, as much as to say to him, "Get out of my sight, you son of a doorkeeper! You want to get into the police, you son of a doorkeeper? The son of the doorkeeper wants to be an officer? That's a good one, I swear!"

Taha started to pace the room for he had made up his mind that he had to do something. He told himself that he could not remain silent while they humiliated him in this way. Slowly, he started to imagine fantastic scenes of revenge: he saw himself, for example, delivering the generals on the committee a speech about equal opportunity, rights, and the justice that God and his Prophet—God bless him and grant him peace— had bidden us to. He went on rebuking them until they melted in shame for what they had done and apologized to him and announced his acceptance into the college. In the final scene, he saw himself grasping the presiding general's collar and shouting in his face, "What business is it of yours what my father's job is, you cheating bribe-taker!" Then he directed at it a number of violent blows, in response to which the general fell to the ground, drowning in his own blood. It was his habit to imagine scenes like these whenever he found himself in difficult situations that he could not control. This time, however, the scenes of revenge, for all their power, could not assuage his thirst. Feelings of humiliation continued to bear down on him, until an idea occurred to him that he could not get out of his head. Sitting down at the small desk and taking out a piece of paper and a pen, he wrote in large letters at the top of the page, "In the Name of God, the Merciful, the Compassionate. Complaint presented to His Excellency the President of the Republic." He stopped for a moment and tipped his head back, feeling some comfort at the grandiloquence of the words and their solemnity. Then he applied himself diligently to writing.

I have left this space empty because I couldn't think what to write in it:

Words are all right to describe ordinary sorrows or joys but the pen is incapable of describing great moments of happiness, such as those lived by Zaki el Dessouki with his sweetheart Rabab and, despite the unfortunate incident, Zaki Bey will always remember the lovely Rabab with her magical, golden-brown face, her wide, black eyes, and her full, crimson lips when she had undone her hair so that it hung down her back and sat in front of him drinking whisky and caressing him with her provocative voice, and how she excused herself to go to the bathroom and came back wearing a short nightdress, opened to reveal her charms; and he will remember that playful smile of hers as she asked him, "Where shall we sleep?" and the irresistible pleasure that her soft, warm body bestowed on him. Zaki Bey remembers every detail of that superb lovemaking and then suddenly the picture in his head becomes distorted and is violently disturbed, and finally cuts out altogether, leaving behind it a dark emptiness and a painful feeling of headache and nausea. The last thing he remembers is a low sound like the hissing of a snake, followed by a penetrating smell that stung the membranes of his nose, at which moment Rabab started examining him with a strange look as though watching for something. After that, Zaki Bey remembers nothing. . . .

He awoke with difficulty, the hammers of an appalling headache banging on his head, and found Abaskharon standing next to him, showing signs of apprehension and whispering insistently, "Your Excellency is unwell. Shall I call a doctor?"

Zaki shook his heavy head with difficulty, making an extraordinary effort at the same time to gather his scattered thoughts. He thought he must have been asleep for a long while and wanted to know the time, so he looked at his gold wristwatch, but it wasn't there. Nor was his wallet on the table next to him where he'd left it. At this, he knew for sure he'd been robbed and little by little started to make an inventory of what was missing: in addition to the gold watch and the five hundred pounds that were in his wallet, Zaki Bey lost a set of gold Cross pens (unused, in their case) and a pair of Persol sunglasses. The worst blow, however, was the theft of the diamond signet ring belonging to his elder sister Dawlat el Dessouki.

"I've been robbed, Abaskharon! Rabab robbed me!"

Zaki Bey kept repeating this as he sat almost naked on the edge of the couch that shortly before had been a cradle of love. At that moment, in his underwear and with his frail body and empty, collapsed mouth (he had removed his false teeth so as to be able to kiss the Beloved), he looked very much like some wretched comic actor, resting between scenes. Overwhelmed by misery he put his head in his hands while Abaskharon, agitated by this momentous event and excited as a locked-up dog, started to strike the ground with his crutch and pace the room in every direction. Then he bent over his master and gasped out, "Excellency, should we report the bitch to the police?"

Zaki thought a little, then shook his head and remained silent. Abaskharon came closer and whispered, "Excellency, did she give you something to drink or spray something in Your Excellency's face?"

Zaki el Dessouki had needed that question in order to be able to articulate his anger and he flared up, raining insults on the unfortunate Abaskharon. In the end, however, he accepted his help in getting up and dressing, for he had decided to leave.

It was past midnight and the stores on Suleiman Basha had closed their doors. Zaki Bey walked with dragging steps, staggering from the effects of the headache and fatigue, an enormous fury slowly building up inside him. He thought of the efforts and the money that he had spent on Rabab and the valuable things she had stolen from him. How could all this have happened to him? Zaki Bey the distinguished, the woman charmer and lover of noblewomen, tricked and robbed by a low prostitute! Perhaps she was with her lover at this minute, giving him the Persol glasses and the gold Cross pens (unused) and laughing with him at the gullible old man who had "fallen for it."

His ire was increased by the fact that he could not inform the police for fear of the scandal, echoes of which would inevitably reach his sister Dawlat. Likewise he could not go after Rabab or make a complaint against her at the Cairo Bar where she worked since he knew for sure that the owner of the bar and everyone who worked there were hardened criminals with previous convictions and that the robbery might even have been carried out for them. In any case there was no possibility they would support him against Rabab and it was even on the cards that they would beat him up, as he had actually seen them do with disorderly customers.

There was nothing for it therefore but to forget the whole incident, and how difficult and painful that was—not to mention the anxiety weighing on his heart over the theft of his sister's ring. He started blaming himself: when he had got the ring back from Papasian the jeweler's after it was mended, why had he kept it in the office instead of hurrying to return it to Dawlat? What was he to do now? He could not afford to buy a new ring and even if he could, Dawlat knew her jewelry as she did her own children. He feared his confrontation with Dawlat more than anything else—so much so that when he arrived in front of their apartment in Baehler Passage, he stood hesitating at the entrance and it occurred to him to go and spend the night at one of his friends' houses, and this he almost did. But it was late and his exhaustion was driving him to go upstairs, so he went.

"And just where has His Lordship been?"

These were Dawlat's opening words to him as he stepped into the apartment. She was waiting for him in the reception room, on the seat facing the front door. She had wrapped her chestnut-dyed hair on her "*boucles*" and covered her lined face with thick layers of powder, while a lighted cigarette in a small gold holder dangled from the corner of her mouth. She had on a blue house robe that covered her thin body and had stuffed her feet into her "*pantoufles,*" which were shaped like white rabbits. She sat knitting, her hands moving in a quick, mechanical way, never stopping or slackening their pace, as though they were divorced from the rest of her body. Habit had taught her the skill of smoking, knitting, and talking simultaneously.

"Good evening."

Zaki said the words quickly and tried to move on directly to his room but Dawlat launched her attack immediately, screaming in his face, "What do you think you are? Living in an hotel? Three hours I've been waiting for you, to and fro between the door and the window. I was just going to call the police. I thought something must have happened to you. It's too bad of you! I'm sick. Do you want to kill me? Have mercy on me, Lord! Lord, take me and let me rest!"

This was a kind of brief overture to a quarrel in four movements that might stretch out till the morning and Zaki, quickly crossing the hall, said, "I'm sorry, Dawlat. I'm extremely tired. I'm going to sleep and in the morning I'll tell you what happened, God willing."

Dawlat, however, was alert to his attempt at flight and, throwing the knitting needles from her hands, rushed at him screaming at the top of her voice, "Tired from what, you poor thing? From the women you spend all your time sniffing after like a dog? Wise up, mister! You could die any day. When you meet Our Lord, what are you going to tell Him then, *mister?*"

With the last cry, Dawlat gave Zaki a hard shove in the back. He staggered a little but rallied his forces and slipped inside his room, where despite Dawlat's fierce resistance he managed to lock his door, stuffing the key into his pocket. Dawlat continued to shout and rattle the doorknob to make him open up but Zaki felt that he'd made it to safety and told himself that it wouldn't be long before she got tired and went away. Then he lay down fully clothed on the bed. He was tired and sad and he started to review the events of the day, muttering in French, "*Quelle journée horrible!*" Then he thought of Dawlat and asked himself how his beloved sister could have been transformed into this vicious, hateful old woman.

She is only three years older than him and he still remembers her as a beautiful delicate girl wearing the yellow and navy school uniform of the Mère de Dieu and learning selections of La Fontaine's animal verses by heart. In the evenings she would play the piano in the reception room of their old house in Zamalek (which the Basha had sold following the Revolution). She played so well that Mme. Chedid the music teacher approached the Basha about the possibility of her applying for the international amateurs' competition in Paris but the Basha refused and Dawlat soon married Airforce Captain Hassan Shawkat and had a boy and a girl (Hani and Dina). Then the Revolution came and Shawkat was pensioned off because of his close relations with the royal family and soon after died a sudden death while still less than forty-five years of age.

Dawlat remarried twice after him but had no more children—two failed marriages that left her bitter, nervy, and a cigarette smoker. Then her daughter grew up, married, and emigrated to Canada. When her son graduated from the School of Medicine, Dawlat waged a fierce battle to stop him emigrating. She wept and screamed and implored all her relatives to convince him to remain with her but the young doctor, like most of his generation, was sick to despair of the situation in Egypt. He was determined to emigrate and offered to take his mother with him but she refused and was left on her own.

She rented out her flat in Garden City furnished and moved in to live with Zaki downtown and from the first day the two old people had not stopped feuding and battling as though they were sworn enemies. Zaki had got used to his independence and freedom and it had become difficult for him to accept anyone else sharing his life—to accept that he would have to stick to appointed times for sleeping and eating and that he would have to tell Dawlat ahead of time if he intended to stay out late. Her presence prevented him from inviting girlfriends home and her barefaced interference in his most private affairs and her constant attempts to dominate him made her even harder to put up with.

From her side, Dawlat endured loneliness and unhappiness and it grieved her that she should end her life without accomplishments or achievements after failing in marriage and seeing her children leave her in her old age. It provoked her greatly that Zaki seemed in no way like a failing old man waiting for death, but still wore scent and played the fop and chased women. No sooner did she catch sight of him smiling and humming in front of the mirror as he primped his clothes or notice that he was happy and in high spirits than she would feel a resentment that wouldn't subside until she'd picked a quarrel with him and flayed him with her tongue. She attacked his childish ways and whims not from a standpoint based on any moral objections but simply because his clinging to life in this way didn't match her own despair, her fury at him being akin to that felt by mourners at the man who guffaws in the middle of a funeral.

In addition there lay between the two old people all the irritability, impatience, and obstinacy that go with old age, plus that certain tension that develops when two individuals live in too close a proximity to one another—from one using the bathroom for a long time when the other wants it, from one seeing the sullen face the other wears when he wakes from sleeping, from one wanting silence while the other insists on talking, from the mere presence of another person who never leaves you day and night, who stares at you, who interrupts you, who picks on everything you say, and the grating of whose molars when he chews sets you on edge and the ringing noise of whose spoon striking the dishes disturbs your quiet every time he sits down to eat with you.

Zaki Bey el Dessouki stayed stretched out on the bed going over these events and gradually drowsiness started to overcome him. However, his bad day wasn't over yet, for it was not long before he heard, as he lay between sleeping and waking, the grating of the spare key, which Dawlat had known where to find. She opened the door, approached him, and, her eyes wide with resentment and her voice gasping with emotion said, "Where's the ring, Zaki?"

Thus Your Excellency Mr. President will see that your son, Taha Muhammad el Shazli, has suffered injustice and the violation of his rights at the hands of the presiding general of the interviewing committee at the Police College. The Prophet—God bless him and give him peace—has said, in a sound hadith, "Verily, your people who were before you would leave alone a nobleman if he stole, and would invoke the punishment against a poor man if he stole. By God, even if Fatima, daughter of Muhammad, stole, I would cut off her hand."

The Prophet of God has spoken truly. Mr. President, I went to great trouble and made great efforts in order to obtain a score of eighty-nine (Humanities), and I was able, through God's bounty, to pass all the tests for admission to the Police College. Is it then just, Mr. President, that I should be denied admission to the police force for no better reason than that my father is a decent but poor man who works as a property guard? Is not the guarding of property a decent occupation, and is not every decent occupation to be respected, Mr. President? I ask you, Mr. President, to look into this complaint with the eye of a loving father who will never agree that injustice be done to one of his sons. My future, Mr. President, awaits a decision from Your Excellency and I am confident that, the Almighty willing, I shall meet with fair treatment at your noble hands.

May God preserve you as an asset for Islam and the Muslims,
Your sincere son, Taha Muhammad el Shazli
Identity Card No.19578, Kasr El Nil
Address: The Yacoubian Building, 34 Talaat Harb Street, Cairo

Like a victorious wartime general who enters in triumph a city he has conquered after bitter fighting, Malak Khilla appeared on the roof of the building to take possession of his new room in a happy and vain-